D1872089

THE

SPANISH MATCH

OR

CHARLES STUART AT MADRID.

BY

WILLIAM HARRISON AINSWORTH.

Carlos Estuardo soy,
  Que, siendo amor mi guia,
Al cielo de Espana voy
  Por ver my estrella Maria.

LOPE DE VEGA

IN THREE VOLUMES.

VOL. II

LONDON:
CHAPMAN AND HALL, 193, PICCADILLY
1865

CONTENTS OF VOL. II.

BOOK I.—*continued.*

THE JOURNEY OF JACK AND TOM SMITH TO MADRID.

BOOK IV.

FIESTAS REALES.

The Spanish Match.

BOOK I.

(CONTINUED.)

THE JOURNEY OF JACK AND TOM SMITH TO MADRID.

XXI.

THE DUKE DE CEA.

CLOSELY followed by Buckingham and Graham, the two cavaliers marched across the enclosure, and passing through an open gateway, entered the cloisters of the cathedral. The ambulatory was plunged in gloom, so that it was impossible to discern the arched vaultings of the roof, enriched with exquisite tracery, or the many beautiful monuments on the walls. At last the cavaliers came to an opening, where they awaited the arrival of the others, and then the whole party stepped forth into a large quadrangle, which appeared to be laid out as a garden, with a fountain in the centre. The

Spaniards led the way along a gravel walk towards the fountain, which was splashing pleasantly on its marble basin, and, having reached a convenient spot, stood still. The cavalier who had challenged Graham then said:

"Here we can settle our quarrel, señor"

"It is too dark," cried Buckingham. "You will not be able to see each other's swords."

"That objection is easily disposed of," remarked the second cavalier, producing a dark lantern from beneath his cloak, and unmasking it.

"You seem prepared for the emergency, señor," observed Buckingham, in a jeering tone; "but perhaps this lantern was intended to light you to the fair señora."

"It may do so when it has served its present purpose," rejoined the first cavalier. "Hold the lantern, señor, I pray you. You shall not say that any unfair advantage has been taken of your friend. Do you use the capa, señor?" he added to Graham.

And on receiving an answer in the negative, he unfastened his own cloak, and instead of wrapping it round his left arm—a mode of defence then ordinarily practised in Spain—flung it on the ground.

As he did this, Buckingham threw the light of the lantern full upon him, and a tall, slightly-proportioned, and extremely handsome young cavalier was revealed to view. The rich attire of this gallant youth, who could not be more than one-and-twenty, confirmed the assertion he had made as to his rank.

"By my troth, Dick, you have to do with a grandee," said Buckingham. "Harm him not, if you can help it."

"I never meant to hurt him," replied the other.

Meantime, Graham had followed the example of his antagonist, and divested himself of his cloak. Both drew their rapiers at the same moment, saluted, and beat the appeal, carefully watching each other by the light of the lantern, which Buckingham held aloft with a steady hand.

After a few rapid passes, productive of advantage to neither party, Graham, who was a consummate master of fence, felt satisfied that he could bring the conflict to an immediate close, and accordingly, parrying a thrust delivered by the fiery young Castilian noble, he advanced quickly, and before the other could recover, seized the hilt of his rapier with his left hand, and by a strong blow on the blade and a dexterous turn of the wrist, forced the weapon from his grasp.

With a formal bow, he then presented the rapier to his discomfited antagonist, saying:

"Here is your sword, señor, if you desire to renew the fight."

The young Castilian noble took the rapier thus courteously offered him, and immediately sheathed it.

"I should not be worthy of the name I bear if I could use my sword against one who has given me my life," he said. "I own myself fairly vanquished, señor."

"In that case, all hostility between us is at an

end, noble señor," replied Graham. "Permit me to return you the billet which has led to this conflict," he added, taking the letter from his doublet and presenting it to the young nobleman. "You will see that it is unopened. I ought to apologise for having detained it, but——"

"No more, señor—no more, I pray you," interrupted the other. "All apologies should come from me. I was to blame for making the demand so haughtily. You have behaved throughout like a gallant gentleman, and it will delight me to improve my acquaintance with you. I pray you to know me as the Duke de Cea, son of the Duke de Uzeda, and grandson of the Cardinal-Duke de Lerma. This is my friend, Don Antonio Guino."

"I am proud to learn that I have had the honour of crossing swords with the grandson of the great Duke de Lerma, and himself, if I mistake not, a grandee of Spain," replied Graham, courteously returning the salutations addressed to him by the two Spaniards. "Your lordship, I am persuaded, will excuse me if, for the present, I must withhold my own name and that of my friend. I am compelled to do so for reasons the force of which you would recognise if they were mentioned to you. But I may state that we are connected with the English court."

"I am not surprised to hear it," replied De Cea, bowing; "and were I made acquainted with your titles, señores, I doubt not they would be familiar to me. The Conde de Gondomar, late ambassador to England, is my intimate friend, and has often spoken to me of the nobles of your court."

"The Conde de Gondomar is also my intimate friend, duke," said Buckingham; "and I hope to see him on my arrival at Madrid."

"Mil santos! a sudden light breaks upon me," cried the Duke de Cea. "And if I should be right in my conjecture, I shall esteem this meeting one of the most extraordinary events of my life. I am De Gondomar's friend, as I have stated, noble señores, and I believe he has few secrets—even state secrets—from me. I am aware, therefore, that he expects an illustrious personage in Madrid."

"I must set you right on one point, duke," rejoined Buckingham, laughing. "I am not the illustrious personage you refer to, neither is this gentleman."

"But there was a third person with you just now," cried the Duke de Cea, "and he answers so completely to the description I have received from De Gondomar of a certain prince, that I could almost swear 'tis he."

"Without admitting you are right in your surmise, duke," rejoined Buckingham, "I may say that the person you imagine to be the prince desires only to be known as Don Carlos Estuardo. My friend here is Don Ricardo, and I am Don Jorge, at your lordship's service."

"I presume you do not stay long in Burgos, señores?" said De Cea.

"Merely for the night," returned Buckingham.

"I ask, because I have a proposition to make which I trust will not be disagreeable to you," pursued the young duke. "I have been brought to Burgos by the little love affair which you have discovered, but I depart to-morrow morning with my friend, Don Antonio Guino, for Lerma, the castle of my grandsire, the cardinal-duke. Lerma is about half a day's journey hence, and being on the direct road to Madrid, you must needs pass it. It will gratify me exceedingly if you will permit me to attend you thither, and furthermore allow me to present you to the cardinal-duke, who I am sure will esteem himself highly honoured if you will pass the remainder of the day at his castle. Do not refuse my request, I beseech you, señores. It will be a kindness to an old banished minister, who, though he has fallen into unmerited disgrace, and has lost the power and influence he once enjoyed, without a hope of regaining it, still takes the deepest interest in all that concerns his royal master. Your visit will be a consolation to him."

"Thus preferred, it is impossible to refuse the invitation, my lord duke," replied Buckingham, "and I willingly accept it on the part of Don Carlos, who, I am sure, will be gratified to behold a minister so illustrious, as well by his noble actions as by his misfortunes, as the Cardinal-Duke de Lerma."

"It becomes me not to praise my grandsire, noble señor," replied the young duke, in a tone of profound emotion. "He has fallen, and there are few to praise him now. But I can say of him, with truth, that he served the late king, Philip III., faithfully and well. He filled the highest post in this kingdom, just as the Marquis of Buckingham fills the highest post in England; and though disgraced, he committed no act to forfeit his royal master's favour. His enemies triumphed over him. But he bears his reverses with dignity, and without a murmur, and is greater now than when in the plenitude of power."

"Your warmth does you honour, my lord," said

Buckingham. "The great Duke of Lerma deserves all you have said of him. His acts as a minister are remembered in England, though they seem to be forgotten in the country which has so largely benefited by them."

"I shall not fail to repeat your words to my grandsire, noble señor," returned De Cea. "Your visit will give him new life, and recal him for a time to the world from which he has withdrawn. But I will not keep you longer here," he added, putting on his cloak. "With your permission, Don Antonio and myself will attend you to your hotel."

"Do not trouble yourself further about us," said Buckingham. "We can easily find our way to the parador where we are lodged."

"Nay, I must insist upon escorting you thither," said De Cea. "And I trust you will honour me by a presentation to Don Carlos."

Buckingham readily assenting, the whole party quitted the cloisters, animated by very different feelings from those which they had experienced on entering them, and made their way past the cathedral to the plaza in which the parador was situated.

Arrived there, Buckingham had a few words in private with Charles, and briefly explained what had occurred. The Duke de Cea and Don Antonio were then presented to the prince, who received them both very graciously, and professed himself delighted at the prospect of beholding the Cardinal-Duke de Lerma on the morrow.

"I am infinitely obliged to you, my lord duke," he said, "for the opportunity you are good enough to afford me of beholding so distinguished a personage as your grandsire."

"You are too good, señor," returned De Cea, bowing low. "The obligation is entirely on my side."

Charles then pressed the duke and his friend to stay and sup with him, but they respectfully begged to be excused, and Buckingham came to the rescue, significantly observing, "Do not urge the duke further. I know he is better engaged."

"Nay, then I will say no more," remarked Charles, smiling. "Will it be agreeable to your lordship to start so early as eight o'clock to-morrow morning?"

"It will suit me perfectly," replied De Cea. "After matins, which I have promised to attend at the cathedral, I shall be perfectly free."

"Do not hurry yourself, duke," laughed Buckingham. "We will wait for you."

De Cea and Don Antonio then took their departure, and shortly afterwards Charles and his attendants sat down to supper.

XXII

HOW THE DUKE DE CEA MADE A CONFIDANT OF DON RICARDO.

At a very early hour next morning, Charles, accompanied by Buckingham and Graham, repaired to the cathedral.

The full beauties of the superb Gothic fane were now revealed to them—the tall twin spires cleaving their way towards heaven, the three exquisitely carved portals of the grand entrance, the triple-shafted aisles, the majestic nave, the vaulted roof, the numerous chapels with their monuments, statues, and paintings, the magnificent choir with its splendidly gilt gates, beautiful stalls, and glorious canopy—all these, and a thousand beauties more, were displayed to their ravished gaze. To complete their satisfaction, the grand notes of the organ were heard pealing along the roof, while sweet voices arose from the choir.

As on the previous evening, the pavement of the mighty nave was peopled with female devotees, all producing a singular and striking effect, from their black attire, their fans and mantillas; and many of them—the younger at least—boasting magnificent eyes, jet-black locks, and charming features. In the chapels also there were many worshippers; and though the hour was so early, the cathedral might be said to be thronged.

As Graham passed the chapel of Santa Ana he could not help casting a glance into it, and then perceived the beautiful creature he had seen there on the previous night. She was kneeling before the image of the Virgin, and not far from her stood the young Duke de Cea, so engrossed by the contemplation of his divinity, that he had eyes for no other object.

Charles remained within the cathedral for more than an hour, chiefly employing himself in examining the many marvellous paintings which he had been unable to inspect on the previous evening, and then, deeply deploring the necessity of departure, he bade adieu to the glorious pile, in which he would willingly have tarried during the whole of the day, and returned with his companions to the parador, where breakfast awaited them.

"I do not think the Duke de Cea will be punctual to his appointment, for I saw him in attendance upon a fair señora as we quitted the cathedral," observed Buckingham, helping himself to a cup of chocolate, which formed the staple of the frugal repast.

"I venture to differ with your lordship," said Graham. "It still wants a quarter to eight. In my opinion, he will be here at the hour agreed on."

Graham was right. Before the cathedral bell tolled eight, the Duke de Cea and Don Antonio, each mounted on a superb Barbary horse, and attended by a couple of lacqueys in rich liveries, likewise well mounted and well armed, rode into the court of the parador.

As they alighted, Charles and Buckingham came forth to meet them, and naturally expressed admiration of their beautiful barbs.

"I am glad you like them," said the young duke. "Though full of fire, they are as easy to sit as a lady's palfrey, and might be reined by a silken thread. You will confer a favour upon me by accepting them."

"Impossible!" exclaimed Charles.

"Do not mortify me by a refusal, noble Don Carlos," cried De Cea. "Keep one yourself, and give the other to Don Jorge."

It was so evident that the generous young noble would have been deeply hurt by a refusal, that Charles could not say nay, but, mounting the barb proffered him, found that the noble animal had all the qualities ascribed to him. Buckingham required no further solicitation, but immediately vaulted into the saddle of the other Barbary courser, which was resigned to him by Don Antonio, and was enchanted with his acquisition.

At this moment a bevy of mules, ready saddled and bridled, was brought out, and as if to prove the value of De Cea's present, the vicious brutes made a most horrible disturbance, kicking, squealing, shrieking, and biting furiously, like wild beasts. Some time elapsed before the refractory animals could be mounted. At last, however, amid a hurricane of imprecations from the postilions, the cracking of whips, and the shrill cries of the mules, whose tough leathern hides resounded with oft-repeated blows, the cavalcade got into motion, and made its way across the plaza, and along several narrow streets abounding in churches, convents, and ancient and picturesque habitations, and swarming with muleteers, priests, friars of various orders, and dark-eyed women draped in mantillas.

At the head of the company rode Charles, with the young Duke de Cea by his side, and the latter called the prince's attention to several remarkable structures as they passed along.

"'Tis a thousand pities you are obliged to quit Burgos without visiting the house of the Cid, and his tomb at the convent of San Pedro de Cardeña," observed the duke.

"Time is wanting," replied Charles. "I reverence the memory of the great Gothic hero, but I must be content with beholding the city wherein he dwelt, the proudest recollections of which will ever be associated with his name."

Making an exit from Burgos by the Arco de Santa Maria, the troop traversed a bridge over the Arlanzon, and when half way across, the Duke de Cea called a momentary halt, and directed the prince's attention to the beautiful gate through which they had just passed, and which was decorated with statues of the Cid, Fernan Gonzalès, the Emperor Charles V., and other renowned personages.

From this bridge a magnificent view of the city was obtained, with its lordly castle and superb cathedral towering above the other structures. The twin spires and central tower of the splendid fane, now displayed in all their beauty, again excited the enthusiastic admiration of the travellers. It was with a sigh that Charles gave the word to the cavalcade to move on, and he more than once looked back at those marvellous spires, which continued in sight long after Burgos itself had disappeared.

The country on which they had now entered was bare and uninteresting, and consisted of parched-up plains, with scarcely an object on which the eye could dwell with pleasure, stony mountains, and miserable villages.

At the solitary venta of Madrigalejo, where they halted, they were treated with profound respect by the host, who, as soon as he beheld the Duke de Cea, proceeded to clear his house of a band of muleteers by whom it was invaded, and then besought his more important guests to enter. Proceeding to the comedor, or dining-hall, they discovered on the table a puchero, a ragoût of rabbits, with a mess of boiled chickens and rice, and their ride having given them an appetite, they immediately fell to work on these viands, and in a short time very little was left for the muleteers, for whom the dishes were originally prepared. Having wound up their repast with a few flasks of excellent valde-peñas, they ordered their horses, and a relay of mules being brought out for those who required them, the party proceeded on their journey, much to the satisfaction of the muleteers.

Buckingham having now joined the prince at the head of the troop, the Duke de Cea fell back, and rode beside Graham. A friendship had already been established between these two young men, whose tastes proved to be perfectly congenial, and ıfter they had conversed together for some time ɔn indifferent topics, De Cea said to his new 'riend:

"I know you to be a man of honour, my dear Don Ricardo, and I will, therefore, unbosom myelf to you, and give you some particulars of the ove-affair in which I am engaged, and with which 7ou have been so strangely mixed up. I need not lescribe the lady, for you have seen her, and know ıow lovely she is. Yes, Doña Flor is very beauiful," he added, with a passionate sigh. "I have een none to compare with her, unless it be her ister. The first moment I beheld her I fell despeately in love."

"I am not surprised at it, duke," remarked Graham. "Like myself, I perceive you are of an nflammable temperament."

"I have often been in love before, Don Ricardo, ut this is a grand passion," said De Cea, with nother sigh, "and threatens to consume me. I an think only of Doña Flor. I must tell you she is married — married to a grandee — Don Pompeo de Tarsis."

"I hope Don Pompeo is old," observed Graham.

"He is under thirty, and remarkably handsome," replied the duke; "but he has a dreadful temper, and Doña Flor detests him. Though perfectly aware of her dislike, he is foolish enough to be jealous."

"Apparently not without cause," remarked Graham. "Permit me to inquire whether Don Pompeo resides in Burgos or the neighbourhood?"

"He has a mansion in Burgos," replied De Cea. "But he lives chiefly in Madrid, or Valladolid, as he belongs to the court. He is in Madrid at this moment, and you are certain to see him on your arrival, for he is in great favour with the minister, the Conde de Olivarez."

"How comes it, if he is as jealous as you represent him, that he allows his wife to be alone in Burgos?" inquired Graham.

"She is under the care of a dueña and an old servant, who are watchful as dragons," replied De Cea.

"But you have found out a way to put the dragons to sleep—eh, duke?"

"I have gained over the dueña, but not old Basilio. He is incorruptible," replied De Cea. "But, nevertheless, I have ventured to follow Doña Flor to Burgos, and in spite of Basilio's vigilance, by the aid of a rope-ladder have contrived to obtain more than one interview with her."

"But why quit Burgos, if she remains there?" asked Graham.

"It would be useless to stay. I could not see her again. To-day she expects the arrival of her father, the Conde de Saldana, who is travelling from Vittoria to Madrid."

"Heavens!" exclaimed Graham. "Then Doña Casilda is her sister."

"She is," replied De Cea, in equal surprise. "Is it possible that you know Doña Casilda?"

"You shall hear," said Graham. And he proceeded to recount his adventure with the bandits in the gorge of Pancorbo.

"By the black eyes of her I love, this is most strange and incredible!" exclaimed the young duke. "You are a fortunate man, Don Ricardo. Doña Casilda cannot be ungrateful after the important service you have rendered her. But you must not lose time. I rather think her father has promised her hand to Don Christóbal de Gavina."

"Diablo!" exclaimed Graham, in a tone of vexation.

"Moreover, I cannot disguise from you that Don Christóbal is young, handsome, and rich—he has mines in Mexico—so you see you have a formidable rival. But do not despair, amigo. I know the impulsive nature of my countrywomen, how quickly they are captivated by gallantry and devotion, and I am certain that the courage you displayed in the encounter with the bandits must have produced a strong impression upon Doña Casilda's susceptible breast."

"But she may have already given her heart to Don Christóbal," said Graham, in a despondent tone.

"I don't think so," replied De Cea. "At all events, you will have the entrée of the Casa Saldana, and can see her as much as you please. The main difficulty will be with the old Conde. If he has promised her to Don Christóbal, he will not break his word. But, after all, love would be a very tame affair without a few difficulties and dangers. I should not be half as much enamoured as I am of Doña Flor if there were no obstacles in the way."

"That may be very true, my dear duke," replied Graham, laughing, "and, to confess the truth, I did not know that Doña Casilda was so important to my happiness as I now find, since there is every probability of losing her."

"Courage! trust to me, and you shall not lose her," cried De Cea.

"Faith! you are a friend in need, my dear duke, and I thank my stars for throwing you in my way."

"Without me you might possibly fail, that I will allow, my dear Don Ricardo," said De Cea. "I know the manners of my country, which no stranger can perfectly comprehend. Nos otros Españoles are a strange people, as you will find, before you have lived amongst us long. I will lay you any wager you please that you will have less trouble with your suit than Don Carlos Estuardo will have with the Infanta."

"Think you so, duke?" cried Graham.

"I am certain of it," replied De Cea. "To say nothing of the difficulties of the negotiation which may possibly be overcome by the presence of Don Carlos, his patience will be worn out by the rigorous etiquette practised in our court, and to which he will be compelled to submit. Unless by stratagem —and if he has recourse to it he will be in great personal peril, and will put half a dozen heads in jeopardy—he will never be able to obtain a private interview with his mistress. When they are together in public, she will be as cold to him as the ice of the Sierra Nevada. A princess of the royal blood of Spain is the slave of form. She is brought up in it, till it becomes part of her nature. She can only act, move, think, and talk, as etiquette prescribes. As jealously guarded as a Moorish princess, she cannot even stroll in the palace gardens unattended."

"'Sdeath! this will not suit Don Carlos," cried Graham. "He fondly persuades himself that he will pass the best part of each day in his mistress's society."

De Cea indulged in a hearty fit of laughter, and then said, "Dreams—dreams—mere poetical fancies, Don Ricardo. The first interview will dispel the illusion. There is nothing romantic—nothing tender—nothing exciting in a royal courtship in Spain. It is a stiff, formal, insipid—I may say, stupid affair. I will describe what will take place. Cold as a statue, and almost as inanimate, the Infanta will receive her ardent lover—for you say he is ardent — with a frigidity that will at once quell his passion. She will give him her hand to kiss, for that is permitted by etiquette. Etiquette will also allow her to reply—but only in studied terms — to his impassioned address. Then she will become dumb—perfectly dumb—and will presently retire."

"Zounds! duke," cried Graham, "you do not draw a very attractive picture."

"It is not in the slightest degree over-coloured," said De Cea. "I have seen what I describe"

"But is the Infanta Maria really as cold and unimpassioned as you paint her?" asked Graham.

"I do not mean to affirm that. For aught I can tell, there may be a volcano beneath that crust of snow, but Don Carlos will never find it out until she becomes his bride. I hope he may get well through the ordeal. It is more than I could.

Three days of such dull work would annihilate me."

"From what you say, duke, the Infanta Maria cannot resemble her sister, Anne of Austria, who is one of the most captivating creatures I ever beheld, and apparently ardent as captivating."

"Pardon me, amigo. The Infanta Maria exactly resembles her sister. Before her union with Louis XIII., the Infanta Ana was just as formal and precise as her younger sister. Her lovely eyes, now beaming with witchery, were then without lustre. Even after marriage, Louis complained of her coldness, and dismissed her old dueña, the Duchess de Villaquieras, and her camaréra mayor, Doña Luisa Osorio, both of whom, from their intolerable formality, disgusted his majesty."

"From this you lead me to infer that an equal improvement will take place in the Infanta Maria," observed Graham. "A portrait I have seen of her by Velasquez, which is in the prince's possession, represents her as exceedingly beautiful. But the painter may have flattered."

"Velasquez has not flattered. The Infanta has a charming figure, if it were not too stiff; fine eyes, if she would but use them aright; bright golden tresses, though I prefer locks of a darker shade—such as belong to Doña Flor and Doña Casilda; a complexion dyed like a blush rose—a paler skin is more to my taste; full, ruddy lips, to which I make no objection; and teeth like two ranges of pearls."

"You raise my hopes, duke, which had been cast down by your previous description."

"If Don Carlos has patience, all will be well," observed De Cea, "but he must not imagine that he will meet with a tender reception from his mistress. She will scarcely accord him a smile. And if he should venture to squeeze her hand, she will effectually check the repetition of such an endear-

.ent. You must own that we bring up our prin-
esses strictly in Spain, Don Ricardo, and take
'ery care of them before marriage. They ought
 make excellent consorts—and perhaps they do.
.t all events, it is to be hoped that the future
Queen of England will do credit to her governors
nd governesses."

At this juncture, Don Antonio, who had already
egun to smoke, and had induced Cottington and
ndymion Porter to follow his example, rode up
nd offered them cigars, or tobacco for cigarettes.
.s King James was not present to denounce the
roceeding by a "counterblast," and as Charles did
ot share in his august father's abhorrence of the
'agrant weed, Graham gladly accepted the offer—
 did De Cea, and so did the prince and Buck-
ngham. Consequently, in a few minutes after-
'ards, the whole troop was smoking, since long
efore this the lacqueys and postilions had lighted
ieir pipes; the latter, indeed, had begun to blow

a cloud before they left the venta of Madrigalejo.

In this manner, and with discourse such as we have detailed, the party beguiled many a long league, until about mid-day they approached the vast and magnificent castle of Lerma.

XXIII.

OW DON CARLOS AND DON JORGE VISITED THE CARDINAL-DUKE DE LERMA.

BUILT about twenty years before the period of ur story, when its illustrious founder was the ıost important personage in Spain, and could never ave contemplated the reverses that subsequently efel him, the proud Castle of Lerma, from its ıagnitude, commanding position, and splendour, ad an almost regal aspect, well suited to the re-.dence of an omnipotent minister, but little in ccord with the retreat of a disgraced favourite. 'he grandeur and haughty air of the pile looked .ke a mockery of its owner's fallen fortunes.

The stately structure occupied the brow of a hill rising from out a town belonging to the cardinal-duke, and from which he derived his title, and commanded extensive views over plains watered by the Arlanza. The whole country within view of the castle, and much beyond it, had once belonged to the Duke de Lerma, but the greater part of his vast possessions had been confiscated, and little more than a tithe of his princely revenues was left him. Still the castle was kept up with a splendour befitting the dignity of the cardinal-duke, and the number of his retinue was but little diminished.

Thus, when the cavalcade was conducted by the Duke de Cea through a lofty gateway, sculptured with the armorial bearings of the house of Roxas y Sandoval, into a spacious court, there issued forth a host of lacqueys in sumptuous liveries, headed by a very important-looking mayor-domo. These lacqueys assisted the travellers to dismount, and by the time they had done so a number of grooms f the stable appeared, who took charge of the ıorses.

After a few words had passed between the Duke e Cea and the pompous mayor-domo, the latter ıade a profound bow to Chaıles and Buckingham, nd then ushered the party into the castle, march-ıg before them through a grand entrance-hall full f statues, up a splendid marble staircase, and along corıidor which led to another wing of the edi-ce, where the state bedrooms were situated.

On reaching this wing, the mayor-domo as-gned splendid chambers, each having a couch laced in a deep alcove, to Charles and Bucking-am, and other rooms scaıcely less spacious to Gra-am and the others. The windows of these rooms ›oked out into a charming patio filled with orange-:ees, and having a fountain in the centre.

Meanwhile, the Duke de Cea had disappeared, aving gone to inform the cardınal-duke of the rrival of the visitors. As De Cea had anticipated, is grandsire was overjoyed by the announcement, and, almost with tears in his eyes, thanked him for the gratification he had procured him.

About an hour later, when the guests had refreshed themselves after their journey, and partaken of a collation, the mayor-domo entered, and, addressing Charles and Buckingham, said that his Eminence was impatient to behold them, and prayed them to come to him, as he was unable to leave his room.

On this they both arose, and, attended by the Duke de Cea, followed the mayor-domo, who led them to a suite of apartments on the ground floor. When they had traversed a large audience-chamber, ornamented by portraits of the Emperor Charles V., Philip II., and his son, the late King of Spain, and where several persons were waiting for admission to his Eminence, all of whom bowed deferentially as they passed by, the door of an inner room was opened for them by an usher bearing a white wand, and they were introduced by this official into the presence of the fallen minister.

They found the cardinal-duke in a large library, the shelves of which were filled with magnificently-bound volumes. He was seated in an arm-chair near a table covered with books and papers, and his legs, enveloped in a mantle lined with miniver, were supported by a velvet footstool. Behind the chair in which he sat was placed a large screen. Two chaplains were with him at the time, but as the prince and the others entered, they bowed respectfully and withdrew. The usher also retired as soon as he had performed his office, and the cardinal-duke was left alone with his visitors and his grandson.

Though but the wreck of what he had been, the once superb Francisco de Roxas y Sandoval was still a very striking-looking person. As Marquis de Denia, and equerry to the Infante Don Philip, in the days of Philip II. he was accounted the handsomest man of the court. His stately form was now bent, and he was almost deprived of the use of his lower limbs by gout, but he still possessed remarkable dignity of manner, and his features, though stamped by age, and bearing traces of care and suffering, were noble in expression. The outline of his face was as regular as it had been in youth. His pointed beard and moustaches were white as snow, but his brows were black and bushy, and gave great effect to the glances of his keen, penetrating eyes. He wore a scarlet cassock with a cape of miniver, and had a red silk calotte on his head. From his neck was suspended by a blue riband the cross of Santiago. Such was the personal appearance of this distinguished man. His manner combined dignity and affability in an uncommon degree, and may be described as at once courtly and captivating. He could not rise to receive his visitors, who were presented to him by the Duke de Cea, but apologised for the inattention, and besought them to be seated near him.

"Pardon me if I gaze on you too earnestly, prince," he said to Charles, "but I cannot take my eyes from your countenance. One of the chief wishes of my life is now gratified—gratified when least expected. I desired to behold you, and Heaven has granted my prayer. From the bottom of my heart I thank you for the visit. It is a proof of a generous nature that you do not neglect the unfortunate."

Charles having made a suitable reply to this address, the old man turned to Buckingham, and said, "To you, also, my lord marquis, I must express the great satisfaction I feel at seeing you beneath my roof. I cannot receive you as an equal, for you are in power, and I am not. But I am deeply sensible of the honour you confer upon me. I am the more touched by this visit, because I have reason to fear that it will give umbrage to the Conde de Olivarez, and through him to the king."

"The prince would not be deterred by any such consideration from visiting your Eminence—neither would I," rejoined Buckingham.

"I am infinitely beholden both to the prince and to yourself, my lord," said De Lerma. "But it will pain me if my apprehensions should prove correct. And now, prince," he continued, "suffer me to offer my tribute of admiration to the extraordinary gallantry you have displayed in this enterprise—a gallantry worthy of the best days of chivalry, and which, if there be any of the spirit left that used to animate our nation, must obtain its reward. The Infanta must appreciate a devotion without parallel since the age of knight-errantry. Our young king cannot be insensible to the confidence placed in him, and must turn a deaf ear to the counsels of his minister, who alone has delayed the match. That you have adopted such a step bespeaks a courageous and noble heart. But you have done well. We Spaniards adore gallantry, and when the news of your arrival amongst us becomes known, it will excite universal enthusiasm. The whole people will hail you as the lover of their princess, and will demand with one voice that she be given to you."

"I sincerely trust your prediction may be fulfilled, lord cardinal," said Charles.

"Doubt it not, most noble prince," cried De Lerma, his pale and furrowed cheek flushing, and his eye kindling as he spoke. "I should blush for my country, and would forswear allegiance to my king, if it were not so. But Philip, though he has ill counsellors, has a noble heart, and will act rightly."

"He will, if the Conde de Olivarez will only let him," remarked De Cea.

"Throughout the negotiations we have distrusted Olivarez, my lord," said Buckingham.

"And with reason," rejoined De Lerma. "He is the sole obstacle I now discern, for the prince's gallant conduct will have removed all others. Oh! for one hour of my former greatness! The match should then be speedily brought about. Were I, as I once was, the king's chief counsellor, I would say to him, 'Sire, the step taken by the Prince of Wales in coming to us in person, almost without escort, to claim his bride, must be met in a kindred spirit. Delays must be at an end. With or without a dispensation from the Pope, we must give him the Infanta.' And all Spain would ratify my decision."

"In the name of all Spain, I beg to express my entire concurrence in your Eminence's opinion," said his grandson. "The prince ought to have the Infanta, and *shall* have her, in spite of Olivarez."

"I would you were still in power, lord cardinal," said Charles.

"I could serve your highness, my king, and my country at the same time, if I were so," replied De Lerma.

"Few ministers have maintained their position so long as you, my lord," observed Buckingham.

"True, and at the moment when I deemed myself most secure I was stricken down," rejoined De Lerma. "I am as notable an instance of the instability of greatness as your own Cardinal Wolsey. The highest post of this realm was conferred upon me by Philip III., who reposed entire confidence in me, and committed the reins of government to my control. I was then absolute master of the destinies of the kingdom, and laboured zealously—and I trust well—for the glory of my sovereign and the welfare of my country. I cannot reproach myself with any act of oppression or injustice. I distributed favours with a lavish hand, and sought to conciliate my numerous enemies by moderation and kindness. I could readily have freed myself of them by other means. Like your august and sagacious sire, prince, I sought to maintain peace, and succeeded in doing so during my lengthened term of power. Though the royal coffers needed replenishment, I exacted no heavy tributes, and enforced no intolerable imposts. Hence the people loved me—and some few, perchance, love me still."

"Many—very many!" cried his grandson.

"I hope so," rejoined the old man, "for I have striven to earn their love. I encouraged agriculture, too much neglected with us since the discovery of the New World, and gave rewards for successful industry. I reconciled the internal troubles of the kingdom, and my crowning triumph was the pacification of Aragon. I was then at the acme of my greatness. The wealth of Spain was at my disposal. No request of mine would have been refused by the king, and if it be a fault to enrich and aggrandise my family, I committed it. Lands and titles were pressed upon me by the king. I made my son a duke and a grandee of Spain. I also made his son, who stands before you, a duke and a grandee. I bestowed large possessions upon the Duke de Uzeda. I did more, I earnestly recommended him to the king, who gave him a portion of the favour which he had hitherto bestowed exclusively on me. Alas! I found a traitor in my own son."

"Proceed no further with your story, I pray you, my lord," implored De Cea.

"Nay, I must speak out, Guzman, or my heart will burst," said the old man, with much emotion. "Be content. You have never forfeited my love. I have forgiven your father for the grievous wrongs he has done me, but I cannot forget them. Let me make an end. Like the great Emperor Charles V., I had ever contemplated passing the latter part of my days in religious seclusion, and being then in a position to ask a cardinalate from the See of Rome, I obtained the dignity. But this acquisition was made the means of causing a breach between me and the king, and finding my influence decline, my enemies rose up against me. At their head was the Duke de Uzeda—my treacherous son. He had undermined me with the king. My enemies prevailed. I was dismissed, and the Duke de Uzeda—I will call him son no more—succeeded to my post."

"I wonder not at your anger, my lord," remarked Charles.

"Thus much I could have borne, for I was tired of the world, but what followed was harder to bear," pursued the old man. "Dismissal was not enough. I might be recalled, and therefore my reputation must be blasted."

"But not by your son, my lord—not by your son?" cried Charles, indignantly.

The Duke de Cea would have interposed, but the cardinal-duke checked him.

"I will not be interrupted," he said, sternly and authoritatively. "I will finish my recital. Terrible accusations were brought against me, and I was even charged with poisoning the Queen Margarita. My secretary, Don Rodrigo de Calderon, was seized, imprisoned, tortured, and finally ɪeheaded, and if my enemies had dared to strike he blow, I should have shared his fate."

"It was my father saved you," cried De Cea, hrowing himself at his grandsire's feet. "Wrong .im not by the thought that he desired your death. Ie averted the blow."

"Heaven alone knows the secrets of his heart. cannot read them," said the cardinal-duke. "Be ıs offences towards me what they may, I have ɔng since forgiven them, but I will never see him ɑore."

"Oh! say not so, my lord," implored De Cea. ' He longs to ask your forgiveness."

"I will never see him again—not even at the ɑst," rejoined De Lerma. "Rise, Guzman. I ɪave no fault to find with you."

Both Charles and Buckingham were too deeply mpressed with what they had heard to make any emark, and for some minutes there was a pro-ɓund silence.

It was broken by the cardinal-duke, who, by a strong effort, recovered his calmness.

"I must entreat your highness to pardon me," he said, turning to the prince. "I have talked too much about myself and my misfortunes. But I thought it might interest you to hear the story of a fallen minister of Spain from his own lips. I do not attempt to defend myself, save from the foul and false accusations that have been brought against me. The acts of my administration speak for themselves. I have been justly punished for my pride and presumption, and humbly bow to the decrees of Heaven."

It was perfectly clear, from the tone in which the latter part of this speech was uttered, as well as from the old man's looks, that his professions of resignation were heartfelt, and consequently they produced a profound impression on his auditors.

"I did not expect such a lesson as I have received from you, my lord," said Charles. "I shall lay to heart the words that have fallen from you, ıd try to profit by them. You have taught me ɔw to behave under adveısity."

"Heaven shield you from it, prince!" exclaimed ıe old man, fervently. "Heaven shield you! Then you ascend the throne of England, may ɔur reign be long, prosperous, and happy!"

"Your history is worth all the homilies I have eard preached against ambition, my lord," said uckingham. "Be sure I shall not forget it."

"May it never be necessary for your lordship recal it!" said De Lerma. "I have found com-rt and consolation in ıeligion, from which source one they are to be derived. Your eyes are yet azzled by power. But I know its nothingness."

Again theıe was a pause, for the solemnity of ıe old man's words impressed silence upon his eareıs, and as they raised their eyes towards him, ıey perceived that his hands were clasped to-ether, and from the movement of his lips they new that he was silently praying.

When he had done, thinking he had intruded

sufficiently long upon him, Charles rose to withdraw. De Lerma did not oppose the prince's departure, but said to him:

"My age and infirmities will not allow me to attend upon your highness as I desire. But I commit you to the care of my grandson, who will exercise the rites of hospitality towards you in my behalf. Attend upon the prince, Guzman, and see that his highness lacks nothing."

Bowing reverently to the old man, Charles quitted the room with De Cea. Buckingham would have withdrawn at the same time, but De Lerma begged him to remain.

From the interview that ensued between them, Buckingham derived much valuable information respecting the court he was about to visit. In depicting the characters of the young king Philip IV. and of the Conde de Olivarez, De Lerma displayed an acuteness and power of observation that astonished his auditor, who rose with a very high estimate of the ex-minister's abilities.

"Beware of Olivarez," said the cardinal-duke. "He is my enemy, and because he is so, you may think I judge him harshly when I say he is treacherous and perfidious, but you will find I am right. He will feign to be your friend—distrust him. He will pretend to promote the match—but be sure that he is secretly opposed to it, and will prevent it if he can. If you can baffle him, you will carry your point; if not, the prince will have taken this journey in vain, and will go back without his bride."

"I shall not fail to profit by your Eminence's counsel," said Buckingham, rising. "I have trespassed too long on your time."

"Not so, my good lord," said the old man. "I never meddle now with state affairs, and indeed I had resolved never to do so again, but as I am sure this match will be advantageous to my country, and as Heaven has brought you and the prince before me, I should not be a true Spaniard if I did not aid you. Once more, be on your guard against

Olivarez. He is as subtle and as deceitful as the enemy of mankind. I know him. With this caution I have done."

So saying, he rang a small silver bell, and the summons being immediately answered by the usher, Buckingham kissed the thin hand extended to him, and retired.

On inquiring for the Duke de Cea, Buckingham was conducted by the mayor-domo to a noble picture-gallery, where he found him with the prince and the rest of the party, who were examining the paintings by Ribera, Zurbaran, Antonio Moro, Juan de las Ruelas, and other masters of the Spanish school, that decorated the walls. A magnificent portrait, by Sanchez Coello, of De Lerma, taken when the duke was minister to Philip II., greatly interested the beholders. They could not help contrasting the tall and stately figure there represented, proud as Buckingham's own, with that of the bent and infirm old man whom they had just quitted.

When the party had sufficiently examined the treasures of the picture-gallery, they proceeded to the tennis-court, the stables, and the orange-garden, and lastly walked forth upon a noble terrace, commanding an extensive view of the plains watered by the river Arlanza. Here they strolled to and fro till summoned to dinner by the mayor-domo.

In the evening the whole party attended vespers in the beautiful and richly-decorated chapel of the castle. The cardinal-duke was present, having been carried thither in his chair. As he was brought out, at the conclusion of the service, Charles and Buckingham took leave of him, and received his benediction.

That night the prince and the marquis were lodged in a manner more suitable to their rank than they had been since they quitted New-Hall. The couches provided for them were so luxurious, so different from the hard beds to which they had been accustomed of late, that they were both unwilling to arise when called, according to arrangement, at an early hour.

Having partaken of a sumptuous breakfast, the whole party repaired to the court, where their horses and mules awaited them. The Duke de Cea and Don Antonio Guino insisted upon accompanying them as far as Aranda del Duero, and all the party having mounted, Charles and his attendants quitted, with regret, the castle, where they had been so hospitably entertained.

XXIV.

EL CORTEJO.

The morning was splendid, and gave an almost smiling aspect to the sterile plains they had to traverse. Having obtained fresh mules at Gumiel de Izan, they pursued their course, and at last reached Aranda, a picturesque-looking town, built on the banks of the renowned river Duero, and surrounded by vine-clad hills, one of which was crowned by a sanctuary dedicated to the Virgen de las Viñas.

Making their way through a narrow street running between overhanging houses, with large balconies, many of which were graced by dark-eyed donzellas, they entered the market-place, which presented a curious spectacle, being crowded by country folk in quaint dresses.

Here they alighted at a posada, and after an hour's rest the prince and his attendants took leave of De Cea and Don Antonio.

"Adios, amigo," said De Cea to Graham, as the latter bade him farewell. "We shall meet again shortly in Madrid. If I should see Doña Casilda and the old Conde, you may rely on my zeal in your cause. Vaya usted con Dios!"

Quitting Aranda by a bridge over the Duero, the banks of which were fringed with trees, and tracking a long and pleasant avenue of Lombardy poplars, the travellers entered upon a tract of country which was little better than a desert. Very wearisome was the journey through this barren district, and Graham sadly missed the lively companionship of De Cea.

As evening came on they approached the Somosierra—a lofty and rugged cordillera separating the two Castiles. As these mountainous passes had an ill reputation, and the travellers had been warned by the Duke de Cea against crossing them at night, the party put up at Cerezo de Abajo, a village situated on an acclivity of the lower part of the sierra.

In the comedor of the venta at which they obtained accommodation, the travellers found a captain of arquebuzeros and his lieutenant, both handsome, active-looking young men, though small of stature.

The host took care to intimate that Captain Mendez and Lieutenant Roque, as he styled them, were engaged in clearing the mountain passes from robbers, and he recommended the travellers to obtain their escort on the morrow.

"The captain has a dozen mounted arquebuzeros with him," he said, "and can see you safely across the mountains, if he is so inclined. How say you, captain?" he added to Mendez. "Will you escort the caballeros?"

"Readily, if they desire it," replied the captain, courteously. "Command me, gentil caballero," he added, bowing to Charles. "Myself and my men are at your service."

"A thousand thanks, captain," replied Charles, "but we will not trouble you. We are well armed, and do not fear attack."

"Take my advice, and don't refuse a good offer, señor!" cried the host. "You may be well armed, but the salteadores won't give you a chance of fighting. They lie in ambush behind the rocks, and the first intimation you will receive of their presence will be a shower of bullets. Besides," he added, with a significant gesture, "El Coitejo is now in the mountains."

"El Cortejo!—who is he?" inquired the prince.

"If you meet him, you won't need to ask the

question, señor," said the host. "Captain Mendez will tell you who he is."

"El Cortejo, señor, is a noted salteador," said Mendez. "He was once a caballero—some say a noble — and piques himself upon robbing like a gentleman. He has hitherto escaped me, but he won't do so long, for I have certain information that he is in the Somosierra."

"Ay, there is no doubt he is hereabouts," observed the host, with a sly look. "But don't make too sure of catching him, captain. El Cortejo is far too cunning to allow himself to be trapped."

"What will you say if I bring him here to-morrow night, patron?" remarked Lieutenant Roque, laughing, and slapping the host on the shoulder.

"I shall say you are a brave man, lieutenant," replied the host. "But you won't do it."

"Por las brazas de San Anton! but I will," cried Roque.

"Nay, if you swear it, I will believe you," said the host.

"I have changed my mind, captain, and will avail myself of your escort," said Charles.

"I do not press my services, señor," replied Mendez, "but I think you will be safer with me. You may chance to meet El Cortejo. He has spies in the village—perhaps in this very posada—and may be on the look-out for you. You start betimes to-morrow, I suppose?"

"Soon after six," returned Charles.

"Buen! my men shall be ready."

Meanwhile, supper had been set upon the table by a mozo, consisting of an olla podrida, flanked by a dish of garbanzos and bacon, an estofado of veal, fried sausages, chickens and rice, and a Montanches ham.

To these viands the travellers did ample justice, and before they rose from table they contrived, with the aid of Mendez and Roque, both of whom proved boon companions, to demolish a considerable number of flasks of delicious val-de-peñas—a wine which, the host stoutly asserted, never harmed any man, drink as much of it as he might.

"I shall not put thy assertion to the test, worthy host," said Charles, as he prepared to seek his chamber, while his companions followed his example.

"Buenas nóches, señores!" cried Captain Menlez, with a laugh. "Lieutenant Roque and I are going to have another bottle. Don't let any thoughts of El Cortejo disturb your slumbers."

Next morning, as Charles looked forth from his chamber window, he perceived a dozen men drawn up in the court-yard.

The prince thought they did not look much like archers, but then he was not familiar with the accoutrements of the Spanish soldiery. The troopers he looked upon were wrapped in long russet cloaks, and wore sombreros, and each man had a trabuco slung to his saddle-bow. Moreover, as one of them dismounted, Charles perceived that he had pistols in his belt. They were mounted on mules, but had in charge a couple of horses, ready saddled and bridled, which evidently belonged to their leaders.

On descending to the comedor, the prince found Captain Mendez and Roque, and their frank and well-bred manner dissipated any suspicions which the appearance of the arquebuzeros had inspired.

"You will find my men badly equipped, señor," said Mendez. "But they are all brave fellows, and have seen good service."

By this time the rest of the party had assembled. Chocolate was then served by the mozo, and while Charles and the others were partaking of it, Captain Mendez said to his lieutenant,

"Let six of the men ride on slowly in advance. The others can follow us."

Roque went out at once to issue the order, and presently a trampling in the court announced that the troopers were setting out.

Shortly after the departure of the advanced

uard, Charles and his companions proceeded to he court-yard, where they found their horses and aules in readiness for them. Captain Mendez was n raptures at the sight of the two barbs.

"I am a judge of horses, señor," he said to Charles, "and I vow to Heaven I never saw anyhing like these barbs. They are perfect beauties. I am not rich enough to offer to buy one of them, as I know it to be worth three hundred doubloons, but I envy you the possession of such a treasure."

"Were you to offer me a thousand doubloons I could not sell you this barb, captain," cried Charles, as he vaulted into the saddle. "It was given me by the Duke de Cea."

"The duke must have a high regard for you, señor," remarked Mendez. "Your barb came from the same nobleman, I presume, señor?" he added to Buckingham.

Buckingham replied in the affirmative, and patted the arching neck of the fiery little animal.

"Cielo! what it is to be a duke!" exclaimed Mendez.

Shortly afterwards, the whole party having mounted, the cavalcade quitted the venta, and began to ascend the cordillera.

About a quarter of a league ahead, the advanced guard might be seen climbing the rugged mountain-side. Captain Mendez rode beside Charles and Buckingham. Then came Graham, with Cottington and Porter. These were followed by the postilions, while Lieutenant Roque, with the rest of the archers, brought up the rear.

In this way the troop, which, from its increased numbers, presented a very formidable appearance, proceeded for more than an hour. By this time they had mounted to a considerable height, though they still seemed far from the summit of the sierra. The road was now hemmed in by rocks, and in many places seemed well fitted for a robber ambuscade. All at once, Charles, who a few moments efore had been watching their progress, lost sight f the advanced guard, and asked Mendez what ad become of them. The captain could not tell, ut proposed to ride on quickly and ascertain, and nvited Charles and Buckingham to accompany im. They complied, and the trio soon left the est of the cavalcade at a considerable distance ehind. Still nothing could be seen of the archers, or was any answer returned to the repeated shouts f Captain Mendez.

"What the plague can have happened to them?" e cried. "They cannot have been captured by El Cortejo. Where the devil are you?" he vociferated.

"Here, captain," responded a voice from behind a rock close beside them.

"Soh! I have found you at last 'Tis well! Show yourselves instantly!" cried Mendez.

At this injunction, and as if they had been waiting for a signal, the six arquebuzeros suddenly dashed from behind the rock, and with fierce imprecations and threats surrounded the prince and Buckingham, and presenting their trabucos at their heads, threatened to shoot them if they offered resistance. So far from attempting to check this movement, Captain Mendez drew aside to facilitate its accomplishment.

"Ha, villain!" exclaimed Charles, drawing a pistol and levelling it at Mendez, "thou hast duped us. But thou shalt pay for thy treachery with life."

So saying, he pulled the trigger, but no report followed.

Buckingham likewise tried to fire, but both his pistols snapped.

Mendez laughed loudly and derisively.

"Your pistols have been unloaded, señores," he said. "They will neither harm me nor my men. You are completely in my power. Possibly you guess who I am."

"I know you to be a robber," rejoined Charles.

"I am El Cortejo, señores," replied the captain, bowing.

After a moment's pause, to allow the announcement to produce due effect, he added, "No harm shall be done you—unless you resist; and in that case you will only have yourselves to blame. I have fallen in love with these charming barbs. You shall give them to me. Do so, and I promise you—palabra de honor, señores—that none of your effects shall be touched, and that neither you nor your companions shall be molested."

"What if we refuse?" demanded Charles, sternly.

"In that case," rejoined El Cortejo, changing his tone to one of menace, "I shall still have the barbs, and shall leave my men to deal with you as they think fit, and help themselves to the contents of your alfórjas."

"We had best accept the rascal's proposition,

and give him the barbs," observed Buckingham to the prince. "We are caught in a trap."

"I must beg you to decide speedily, señores," said El Cortejo. "If you allow the rest of your party to come up, I shall not be able to prevent a conflict, and the result will be disastrous to you, for all your fire-arms have been cared for. Will you give me the barbs, or must I take them?"

"Nay, thou shalt have them," cried Buckingham. "And may the devil give thee joy of thy bargain! It cannot be helped. Resistance would be idle," he added, in an under tone, to Charles, who seemed unwilling to comply.

"You are right," murmured the prince; "but it is vexatious to be thus outwitted."

"Better part with the barbs than with our saddle-bags, and, mayhap, with our lives," returned Buckingham. "The knave has got us in his clutches. There is no escape."

"Is the bargain concluded, señores?" demanded

El Cortejo, who had been watching them narrowly.

"I have already said so," rejoined Buckingham.

"A word more, and I have done," returned El Cortejo. "In half an hour we shall reach the summit of the mountain. Just before entering the village of Somosierra, there is a little chapel, dedicated to Nuestra Señora de las Nieves. Arrived there, you shall both dismount, and deliver me the barbs. Pledge me your word to do this, and no harm shall befal you."

Charles and Buckingham gave the required promise.

On this, El Cortejo ordered his men to lower their trabucos and fall back, and the injunction was instantly obeyed.

"Now, señores, I must beg you to ride on with me," he said.

As there was no help for it, the prince and Buckingham obeyed. The brigands followed, so as to cut off all communication between those in front and their friends. At last, after a toilsome ride of half an hour's duration, the summit of the mountain was attained, and ere long the miserable and bleak-looking village of Somosierra came in sight. At the outskirts of the village stood the little chapel mentioned by the robber chief.

On reaching this structure, El Cortejo came to a halt. Whereupon, without a word being said to them, the prince and Buckingham dismounted, and gave him their bridles.

"You are men of honour, señores," he remarked, courteously. "I really am sorry to deprive you of these charming animals. I should be sorry, also, that you should think I had treated you unhandsomely. Such conduct is inconsistent with the character I try to sustain. I therefore offer you, in return for the barbs, my own horse and that of my lieutenant. They are not bad hackneys, and at all events are preferable to mules."

Though sorely annoyed, the prince and Buckingham could not help laughing at the proposition, and accepted it.

Just as El Cortejo had dismounted, and was in the act of delivering his horse to Charles, Graham rode up, and as he stared in astonishment at what was taking place, Buckingham said to him,

"Don Carlos and myself have just made an exchange with Captain Mendez, and have given him our barbs for his horses."

"The deuce you have!" exclaimed Graham, in dismay. "What on earth can have induced you to make such an arrangement? The captain is robbing you."

"I'm sure your friends won't say so, señor," remarked El Cortejo, with a laugh.

"No, no, we are perfectly content. Indeed, we esteem ourselves gainers by the transaction," said Charles, as he sprang on the back of the horse ceded to him by the robber chief.

The next moment, Lieutenant Roque joined the group, and at a word from El Cortejo surrendered his horse to Buckingham, and took possession of the barb. Cottington and Endymion Porter looked completely puzzled, but made no remark.

As soon as El Cortejo had mounted the beautiful barb consigned to him, he said to the prince and Buckingham,

"You will not need my escort farther, señores. There are no robbers on the other side of the Somosierra. Vayan ustedes con Dios."

So saying, he put himself at the head of his band, and, attended by Roque, rode back the way he had come.

"Deuce take me if I can understand it!" mentally ejaculated Graham, as he followed the prince and Buckingham towards the venta. "But I half suspect that the rascal who has just left us is El Cortejo."

XXV.

THE ALCALDE OF CABANILLAS.

DURING the halt of the troop at the venta of omosierra an examination was made, by order of harles, of all the pistols and carbines, when it rned out that the whole of them had been unaded. The cartridges in the bandoliers were kewise empty. No explanation of this alarming scovery was offered by the prince and Buckingam, who likewise maintained a profound silence to what had passed between them and El Corjo.

On quitting the village, the travellers skirted the

snow-covered peaks, which formed the summit of the mountain; and here the cold was intense, but the temperature soon became milder as they descended the southern side of the cordillera. While pursuing their course they came upon a savage-looking pass, where many a murder had been perpetrated, as was shown by the numerous memorial crosses lining the road. However, they passed this "malo sîtio" without being attacked. At Buitrago they obtained a fresh relay of mules, and then pushed on to Cabanillas, a small village at the foot of the lesser mountain chain. Riding up to a venta, Charles inquired of the host, who was standing at the door talking to a couple of travellers, whether he could give them aught for dinner.

"Ay, that I can, your worship," replied the ventero, a fat, merry-looking little fellow. "I can give you as good a dinner as you will get between this and Madrid—an olla podrida, fried trout from the river, poached eggs, and a quisado of rabbit."

"That will do," said Charles. "Let us have the repast with all possible despatch, for we are in haste to proceed on our journey."

"I will order it at once, your worship," replied the ventero, rushing into the house.

As Charles and Buckingham dismounted and gave their horses to a groom, the two travellers, who had been examining the animals with great curiosity, followed the man to the stable.

Meanwhile, Charles and Buckingham, with their attendants, entered the venta and proceeded to the comedor, where they sat down, in anxious expectation of the repast. But more than half an hour elapsed and no dinner appeared, when a considerable bustle was heard outside, and the door was thrown open by the host, who, instead of bringing in the anxiously-expected olla podrida and fried trout, introduced a stout, consequential-looking personage, whom he announced as Don Timoteo del Molino, Alcalde de Cabanillas. The alcalde was attended by a couple of grim-looking alguacils, wearing long black cloaks, and provided with staves. Behind these officers came the two inquisitive travellers previously mentioned, while a number of muleteers, together with the whole household of the venta, male and female, filled up the background.

When the alcalde had got within a short distance of Charles and his companions, who arose to salute him, he called out, "Don Melchior, and Don Geronimo, be pleased to step forward, and prefer your charge against these persons."

"We accuse them of having in their possession two horses, of which we have been robbed by the noted El Cortejo," replied Melchior. "We knew the animals the moment we clapped eyes upon them, but we did not venture to claim them till we had obtained your worship's aid."

"You did perfectly right," replied the alcalde. "Where and when were you robbed of the horses, señores?"

"Two days ago, your worship, between Robre-ordo and Somosierra," replied Geronimo. "Our elief is that all these persons are bandits. It is rue they have the air of caballeros, but then your vorship will bear in mind that El Cortejo affects he manners of a hidalgo, and that several of his and are reported to be ruined spendthrifts of good amily."

"I have heard as much," said the alcalde Now, picaros, what account do you give of your-elves?" he added to Charles.

"We have no account whatever to give," re-urned the prince. "We readily admit that we ad the horses in question from El Cortejo"—(this dmission produced a great sensation, and after it ad subsided the prince went on)—"but if these entlemen can prove their title to them, to your vorship's satisfaction, they shall have them."

"Would you have me understand that your aptain gave you the horses?" demanded the lcalde.

"El Cortejo was obliging enough to give them to us in exchange for a couple of barbs, each of which was worth a dozen such horses," replied Charles.

"Ha! then you mean to assert that you have been robbed by him?" said the alcalde.

"Not being in a condition to reject his terms, señor alcalde, we thought it best to comply with them," rejoined Charles.

"By San Lorenzo, such appears to be the ordinary practice of El Cortejo," cried Melchior. "He gave us a couple of mules in exchange for our horses."

"Very likely the mules were stolen," observed the alcalde.

"Your worship has hit the mark," cried an arriéro, pressing forward. "They were stolen from me. I have just discovered Capitana and Paquita in the stable, and the poor beasts knew me at once."

"Did you receive anything in exchange?" inuired the alcalde.

"Yes, your worship—a miserable donkey," relied the muleteer.

This reply caused much hilarity among the audiors.

"Holy mother! El Cortejo seems to be at the ottom of it all!" exclaimed the alcalde.

"He is the perpetrator of all the robberies in ae Somosierra, your worship," observed the venero.

"All these worthy and honourable persons apear to have been robbed by him," continued the lcalde. "I am at a loss how to settle the matter."

"I will show your worship how to settle it," said Charles. "Let the two gentlemen restore the nules to the arriéro, and they shall have their iorses."

"Por nuestra Señora del Carmen! you have cut he knot of the difficulty, señor," cried the alcalde.

"But I am afraid you won't get back your barbs."

"Not unless your worship can capture El Cortejo, and I fear there is little chance of that," rejoined Charles.

"Sooner or later I shall catch him, señor," rejoined the alcalde. "But it appears to me that this matter is at an end. I presume you are content, señores?" he added to Melchior and Geronimo.

"We have good reason to be so," they replied. "We are greatly beholden to these caballeros, and are sorry to have doubted them for a moment."

And, bowing to Charles and the others, they quitted the room.

"I will go and take possession of Capitana and Paquita," said the muleteer, following them.

The alcalde was likewise about to depart, but Charles begged him to stay and partake of their repast, and the worthy man readily complied. Ac-

rdingly, the grim-looking alguacils were dis-
ssed, and the room being cleared of all intruders, excellent dinner was soon afterwards placed upon e table, to which all the party did justice.

Just as they concluded, the ventero rushed into e room in a state of great excitement, exclaim-
g,

"You have been tricked, señores—shamefully cked!—and so have I. What do you think?—y, you will never guess, so I must e'en tell you those two travellers, who styled themselves Don elchior and Don Geronimo, are rogues and robrs, and so is the arriéro, Pablo."

"What is this you tell us, Tito?" cried the alde, starting up. "Why, you assured me they re honourable men."

"On my conscience, I believed them to be so, ur worship," replied the ventero; "but I have und out my mistake, and it drives me mad to ink I could have been so easily duped. They owe me three dueros for meat, wine, and lodging, and have gone off without paying a single cuarto."

"Have they carried off the horses and mules?" demanded Charles, laughing.

"Ay, plague take 'em! they have, señor," replied the host. "They have galloped off towards the Somosierra, and I hope to San Nicolas they may break their necks on the way. Their parting words to me were, 'Tell the caballeros we are gone to join our noble captain, El Cortejo.'"

"Let us after them, señores!—let us after them!" cried the alcalde. "Bring out your best mules, Tito!—bring out your best mules!"

"It is impossible we can accompany you, señor alcalde," replied Charles. "We must be in Madrid this evening. Obey his worship's order, good host, and bring out your best mules without delay—but they must be for us."

"Well, if you are obliged to depart, señores, no more need be said," observed the alcalde; "and I can only wish you a pleasant journey."

Shortly afterwards, the travellers had mounted ieir mules, and were making their way rapidly :ross the vast arid plain which lay between them id Madrid.

Their next halt was at Fuencarral, and some vo hours later, just as evening was coming on, the alls and towers of Madrid could be distinguished.

Charles uttered an exclamation of joy at the ght, and his enthusiasm and satisfaction were hared by the whole of the cavalcade. For some me no one had spoken, but now every tongue as let loose, and the flagging spirits and energies f the party seemed instantaneously to revive. The iules, too, appeared to participate in the general xhilaration, and, aware that their journey was early at an end, voluntarily quickened their pace, nd soon brought their riders to the gates of the ty.

A certain feeling of disappointment crossed Charles as he gazed at the reddish-coloured mud valls, garnished with Moorish-looking towers and minarets, that rose before him, and he almost involuntarily exclaimed, "Can this be Madrid?"

"Yes, this is Madrid, your highness," replied Cottington, who chanced to be near him; "but you must not judge of the city by its walls, any more than you would fruit by the husk."

"Were the walls ten times uglier than they are, they would be welcome to me as Mecca to the devout Mussulman!" cried Charles "But let us not linger outside. The gate stands invitingly open. Follow me, gentlemen."

Having passed through the archway, the travellers found themselves in a park. A wide road running through it soon brought them to a woody valley, which lay between them and the city. At the bottom of the hollow, extending to some distance on either hand, was a broad open space, wherein was collected a great concourse of well-dressed persons of both sexes, who were promenading to and fro as if in a mall. Cottington informed Charles that this pleasant spot was the Prado.

Though tempted to linger within the Prado, the travellers passed through the gay groups, and mounting the acclivity on the farther side of the woody valley, reached the opening of the splendid Calle de Alcala, which, at this part, might be justly styled a street of palaces.

"At last you are in the 'very noble and very loyal' city of Madrid, as Enrique IV. styled it," remarked Cottington to the prince. "The Madrileños say it is the only capital—solo Madrid es corte. Whether it deserves the distinction, your highness will determine hereafter. Shall we go on? The House of Seven Chimneys is hard by."

Proceeding for a short distance along the Calle de Alcala, the cavalcade, under the guidance of Cottington, diverged into a narrow street on the right, hemmed in by tall habitations, and eventually reached a small plaza, at the farther end of which was a large sombre-looking mansion, flanked on either side by high walls, evidently enclosing a garden. A feature in this house, which instantly attracted the attention of Charles, as well as of such of his attendants as had not previously seen the structure, was its massive and singularly-shaped chimneys.

"Behold it!" cried Cottington, pointing to the mansion. "Behold the House of Seven Chimneys!"

"Let us count the chimneys, and make sure," cried Buckingham. "His majesty desired precise information on the subject. By Heaven! there are only six."

"Count again, my lord," rejoined Cottington, laughing. "Your eyes deceive you. There are certainly seven."

"No such thing!" exclaimed Buckingham, confidently. "I appeal to his highness and to all present whether I am not right. There are two stacks

—and three chimneys in each stack. The house is improperly named."

"We are all of your lordship's opinion," cried those appealed to.

"The designation is perfectly correct," remarked Cottington. "I will back my assertion by any wager your lordship pleases."

"Where, then, is the seventh chimney?" cried Buckingham.

"It is just as visible as the others," returned Cottington.

"To you it may be, but plague take me if I can discern it!" cried Buckingham. "There must be witchcraft in the matter."

"I hope not," observed Charles, gravely. "Give us an explanation of the mystery, Sir Francis."

"That is easily done, your highness," replied Cottington. "It is there," he added, pointing to a cupola in the centre of the building.

A loud laugh, in which all but Buckingham joined, followed this explanation.

"Bah! that is not a chimney," cried the marquis, incredulously.

"Excuse me, my lord, it is the main chimney —la chimenea principal, as the Spaniards say," rejoined Cottington. "There is a curious story connected with that chimney."

"You must find another occasion to tell it, Sir Francis," observed Charles. "We will now enter the house."

"Rightly called, I maintain,—'La Casa de las Siete Chimeneas,'" rejoined Cottington, determined to have the last word.

End of the First Book.

BOOK II.

THE INFANTA MARIA.

I.

THE EARL OF BRISTOL.

WHILE Charles and his attendants were examining the outside of the House of Seven Chimneys, and questioning the propriety of its designation, two persons were seated in a large lofty room on the ground floor at the rear of the mansion.

They had not long returned from the Prado, and their talk was of no very serious or important matters, and chiefly referred to the persons they had met during their promenade. Both of them were very handsome-looking men of middle age, but so different in appearance that it was easy to tell at a glance that one was an Englishman and the other a Spaniard.

In age the Englishman might be about forty-three, and in addition to possessing a tall and graceful figure, and a noble and prepossessing countenance, lighted by keen grey eyes, he had an air of great distinction. His manners were polished and refined, and from his long residence in Madrid and constant intercourse with the court, he had contracted a gravity of look and deportment befitting a high-born and high-bred Castilian. His dark locks, which were cut short, so as to display a well-shaped head and lofty brow, replete with intellect, were streaked with grey, but his pointed beard and moustaches were still black. His doublet and large trunk hose were of brown velvet, and his mantle of the same material. His throat was encircled by a stiffly-starched ruff, and by his side he wore a long rapier. We need scarcely say that this distinguished personage was the Earl of Bristol, then English ambassador extraordinary to the court of Madrid.

Endowed, as we have shown, with remarkable qualifications both of mind and body, John Digby, who was of an ancient Warwickshire family, and nearly connected with the unfortunate Sir Everard Digby, an actor in the Gunpowder Treason, was well qualified to shine at a court like that of James, where personal graces went for so much. Accordingly, when, after spending some years in foreign travel, young Digby was presented to the king, he was very graciously received, and bade fair to become chief favourite. Quickly appointed a gentleman of the privy chamber, knighted, and made a member of the council, Sir John Digby was sent as ambassador to Spain on two occasions—both of which missions he discharged in a very satisfactory manner. Subsequently he proceeded to Germany to negotiate terms of peace for the

Elector Palatine, but though the embassy resulted in failure, its ill success is to be attributed to James rather than his ambassador.

Some years prior to our story, the able and active diplomatist we are describing had been raised to the peerage as Lord Digby, and rewarded for his services by the castle and domains of Sherborne, of which Sir Walter Raleigh had been unjustly deprived; but to give éclat to his fourth and last mission to Madrid, the purpose of which was to treat with Philip IV., then newly come to the throne, for the hand of his sister, the Infanta Maria, he was created Earl of Bristol. On his arrival at the Spanish capital, Bristol, in conjunction with the resident ambassador, Sir Walter Aston, zealously addressed himself to the object of his mission, and, though he encountered numerous obstacles, sufficient progress was made to warrant him in believing that the match would be accomplished. Buckingham, as we have previously shown, hated Bristol,

ıd it was with the design of robbing the ambas-
ıdor of his anticipated triumph, that the favourite
roposed the romantic journey to Madrid, described
ı the foregoing chapters.

We now come to the Spaniard, who was a much
naller man than Bristol, but well made and very
andsome. His complexion was dark, his eyes of
ıe same hue, and his brows and hair jet black. A
ointed beard completed the fine oval of his face.
[is manner was fascinating, but an indefinable
xpression of cunning pervaded his features. His
abiliments, cloak, pourpoint, and hose were of
lack velvet, and well became his graceful figure.
.round his neck he wore the cross of Calatrava.
'his crafty personage was no other than Don
'iego Sarmiento de Acuna, Conde de Gondomar,
ho had been for several years ambassador at the
nglish court, and by his adroit flattery of the
ıonarch, his bribes to the venal courtiers, and his
reat diplomatic skill, had been eminently success-

ful in carrying out the purposes of his mission. Admitted to great familiarity by James, and able to approach him at his festive moments, when he was not entirely master of himself, Gondomar had frequently obtained important secrets from the unguarded king. Believing Gondomar to be devoted to his interests, Buckingham kept up a correspondence with him on his return to his own court. It will be remembered that a private despatch from Gondomar, urging Buckingham to bring the prince to Madrid, decided the favourite upon that course of action. Ostensibly, Gondomar was on excellent terms with Bristol, but he consorted with him chiefly for the purpose of reporting his proceedings to Buckingham.

"It is strange there are no despatches from England," remarked Bristol. "For three days I have looked impatiently for them, but none arrive. I have had no answer to my letter of the 4th February, and yet it required an immediate response."

"No doubt King James cannot make up his ›yal mind, my lord," rejoined Gondomar. "We now he is vacillating in his policy."

"But he leaves me in a state of indecision, hich is very perplexing, and may be prejudicial › our interests," said Bristol. "I speak frankly › you, count, because I know you to be a staunch ıpporter of the match."

"I desire it as much as any Englishman can do -more so, perhaps," remarked Gondomar. "But ıere is no reason for uneasiness. The next intelli- ence you get from England will be satisfactory, epend upon it. Perhaps the courier may have een stopped in the mountains. El Cortejo and is band are in the Somosierra. The last courier rom Paris, who arrived two days ago, was robbed f his letters. Your despatches may possibly be in El Cortejo's possession."

"This is a deplorable state of things, count," aid Bristol—"really disgraceful to the country."

"It is bad enough, I admit," rejoined Gondomar, "but the evil cannot be remedied. We shall always, I fear, have salteadores in our sierras. No sooner is one band exterminated than another springs up. There have always been the Seven Boys of Ecija. If your despatches should not arrive to-night, I will cause a detachment of arquebuzeros to be sent to the Somosierra."

"You are very good, count. His Most Catholic Majesty owes it to his subjects, and to such as enter his dominions, that the highways be kept clear."

"You forget, my lord, that I myself have been robbed on Shooter's Hill, within half an hour of London," replied Gondomar. "I see little difference between your highwaymen and our salteadores, except that the latter are the bolder villains. But let us change the subject. You were not at court to-day. The king noticed your absence, and spoke of it to the Conde-Duque."

"And what said Olivarez?" inquired Bristol, curiously.

"He could assign no cause, but promised to see your lordship to-morrow; so you may prepare for the visit."

"Heaven grant the despatch may arrive in the interim!" cried Bristol. "I am puzzled how to act."

At this moment the door opened, and a young man came in. This was Harry Jermyn, son of Sir Thomas Jermyn, and the ambassador's chief secretary.

"What news, Jermyn?" cried Bristol, eagerly. "Has the courier arrived? Have you got the despatch?"

"No, my lord," replied Jermyn, whose countenance wore a very singular expression, "but a gentleman is without who has ridden post from London."

"Ha! he may bring a letter, or a message from

the king," cried Bristol. "Who is it, Jermyn?"

"He gave a very unpretending name, my lord," replied the young secretary, unable to repress a smile. "He calls himself Tom Smith."

"Tom Smith! 'Sdeath! how should I know him, when there are ten thousand Englishmen so called? Is he a gentleman?"

"He has the air of one, my lord," replied Jermyn.

"Well, admit him."

On this the Conde de Gondomar arose to depart. But Bristol stopped him.

"Stay, count, I pray you," he said. "Tarry at least till I ascertain whether this Tom Smith has any private message for me."

Meanwhile, Jermyn went to the door, and called to the person outside, who instantly marched into the room.

Totally unprepared for such an apparition,

Bristol did not at first recognise the tall figure in travel-soiled habiliments, and funnel-topped boots covered with dust, as that of the magnificent Marquis of Buckingham, but as the so-called Tom Smith advanced, and came more within the light, the truth flashed upon the earl. Better prepared, Gondomar knew the marquis at once.

"My lord of Buckingham!" exclaimed Bristol, greatly astonished. "Do I indeed behold you?"

"Yes, I am here in person in Madrid, my lord, and only just arrived," replied Buckingham.

"You are heartily welcome," said Bristol. "This is a most unlooked-for pleasure. But Jermyn told me you had ridden post from London. Surely he must be wrong?"

"I have ridden every mile of the way, my lord, and I promise you I found it a devilish long journey," rejoined Buckingham.

"I dare say you did," said Gondomar, cordially saluting him. "I am glad you have got here safe and sound, and have escaped the bandits of the Somosierra."

"I can give the last news of them," replied Buckingham. "I have been robbed by El Cortejo. I did not lose much by him, though, and I must say he conducts his nefarious business like a gentleman."

"I have so many questions to ask your lordship, that I scarcely know where to begin," said Bristol; "but my first dutiful inquiries must be in regard to my liege lord the king, and our gracious prince. How fare they both?"

"Both well," replied Buckingham. "The king was in his wonted health when I took leave of him in Whitehall. And as to the prince—why he can speak for himself."

"What! is his highness here?" cried Bristol, in extremity of surprise.

"My brother Jack, who represents him, is in the ante-chamber," replied Buckingham.

"Heaven and earth! can it be? I am lost in wonder!" cried Bristol. "Why did you not tell me this before, my lord? I fly to his highness."

"Stay where you are," rejoined Buckingham. "I will summon him. Prithee come in, brother Jack," he added, calling at the door.

Charles forthwith entered the room. His habiliments and boots, like those of Buckingham, gave evidence of the long journey he had undergone; but his looks did not manifest much fatigue, and his deportment was as dignified as usual.

As he came in, Bristol and Gondomar instantly threw themselves at his feet, and expressed the liveliest satisfaction at beholding him. Thanking them for their welcome in the most gracious terms, Charles raised them, and said to Bristol, with a smile, "You did not expect to see me here, my lord?"

"In truth I did not, your highness," replied the earl. "I never dreamed of such an event. But the unexpectedness of your arrival heightens my joy at beholding you."

"You can guess what brings me to Madrid—eh, my lord?" said Charles, with a glance at Gondomar.

"Your highness can have but one errand," replied Bristol, bowing low.

"Yes, the motive of your highness's journey is easily divined," remarked Gondomar. "The most chivalrous prince in Europe is come in person to claim his bride. Such an act of gallantry and courage, performed by a private gentleman, would excite our admiration—how much, then, must we be moved, when the caballero andante is heir to a throne!"

"Without taking too much credit to myself, count," said Charles, "I may say that the journey has been attended with some little peril, and with some obstructions, as I will hereafter recount to you. I have travelled from London incognito, under the simple name of Jack Smith, and my lord marquis here has played the part of my brother Tom. We have only been known by those names throughout the journey. Our escort has been slight, consisting merely of Cottington, Endymion Porter, and Dick Graham—all of whom are here. As you will naturally suppose, we have had some strange adventures by the way, and, indeed, have courted them rather than shunned them."

"That I can readily believe," remarked Bristol.

"Twice or thrice we have fallen among robbers, and have even been taken for robbers ourselves," pursued Charles; "and to give you an idea of the horses and mules, good, bad, and detestable, that we have ridden, would be impossible. But, on the whole, we have had a merry time of it. Have we not, brother Tom?"

"The merriest three weeks I have ever known,

brother Jack," replied Buckingham. "I am only sorry the journey is at an end."

"I cannot go quite so far as that," said Charles, "but I shall always look back to it with pleasure."

"There is only one thought that mars my delight at beholding your highness," remarked Bristol, somewhat gravely. "Forgive me if I venture to inquire whether this journey has been undertaken with your royal father's sanction?"

"That question, which should never have been asked, my lord," interposed Buckingham, haughtily, "is sufficiently answered by his highness's presence here—and by my presence."

"Make yourself quite easy, my good lord," said Charles, kindly, to Bristol. "I had his majesty's entire sanction for the journey. I have letters from him to yourself, to Sir Walter Aston, and to the king."

"I am glad to receive that assurance from your highness's lips," rejoined Bristol. "Knowing your august father's tender love for you, I could scarcely conceive that he would allow you to incur such risks. I am sure he never consulted the council."

"His majesty felt it to be necessary for the success of his plans that the prince should repair to Madrid," observed Buckingham, with cold significance; "and, being certain that the journey would be opposed by the council, he kept it secret. To me, my lord, he entrusted the precious charge of his son."

"Am I to understand that his majesty is dissatisfied with my conduct?" said Bristol, in a tone that showed how much he was hurt.

"You will understand that henceforward the treaty is under my management," rejoined Buckingham, imperiously.

"Then I am superseded?" cried Bristol.

"You have a master," said Buckingham.

"A master in you, my lord—not so," rejoined Bristol, with equal haughtiness.

"In the prince," said Buckingham.

"I acknowledge his highness," said Bristol; "but you, my lord—never!"

"That remains to be seen," muttered Buckingham.

"A truce to this, my lords," said Charles. "Let not my arrival at Madrid be marked by a misunderstanding between you. You have been overhasty, Geordie. My royal father and myself fully appreciate your services, my good lord," he added to Bristol; "and it is from no distrust of your zeal, either on the king's part or my own, that I have come here. His majesty felt that my presence must bring the matter to a speedy issue. But I shall be guided by your advice."

Bristol bowed deeply, but was too much moved to make any other reply.

"Your highness may command me in every way," said Gondomar to Charles. "I am an Englishman at heart, and will serve you as faithfully as one of your own subjects."

"I shall not hesitate to put your zeal to the test, ount," rejoined Charles. "To-morrow you shall aake known my arrival to Olivarez."

"It will surprise him as much as it has surprised ne," observed Bristol.

"And perhaps be equally displeasing to him," nuttered Buckingham.

"It will gratify me to obey your highness's com-nands," said Gondomar. "I will not venture to predict what will follow the announcement, but I ım sure to-morrow will be a day of rejoicing, such ıs has rarely been witnessed, at our court. And to one person whom I forbear to mention, the news of your arrival will be more welcome than words can tell."

"She ought to be the first to know it," cried Charles, eagerly. "Can it be so managed?"

"The task is difficult and dangerous; but I must prove my devotion to your highness, and I will," said Gondomar. "The Infanta shall know of your arrival to-night. Nay, more, you shall see her, if you are so minded."

"The grand object of my journey will then be accomplished," cried Charles, transported with delight.

"Ah! but you may not be able to exchange a word with her," said Gondomar. "Your highness must consent to be entirely under my control. The slightest imprudence on your part would destroy me. Ask my Lord Bristol, and he will tell you how rigorous are our notions of etiquette, and how great will be the hazard I shall incur."

"Most assuredly you will risk disgrace, count," rejoined Bristol. "Let me dissuade your highness from the step."

"The adventure is too much in accordance with my wishes to be resisted," said Charles. "I will consent to anything, count," he added to Gondomar, "provided I can obtain sight of the Infanta."

In that case you must accompany me to the lace," said Gondomar. "You need make no ange in your attire. When there, I will find u a disguise. I engage that you shall see the fanta, but I rely on your discretion."

"You may entirely rely upon it," rejoined harles

"We will go at once," cried Gondomar.

"Hold, prince!" cried Bristol, throwing himself on his knees, and catching hold of Charles's oak, "I entreat you not to take this rash step. he chances are a hundred to one that you are scovered, and if so, the treaty will be effectually oken. Besides causing a great scandal which n never be forgiven, you will inevitably bring sgrace and ruin on the Conde de Gondomar."

"Do not think of me, your highness," said Gonomar. "I am ready to go with you at all hazards. ou have set us all such an example of courage d gallantry, that we are bound to imitate it. I shall be proud to play a small part in this ro-mantic adventure."

"You will play a very important part in it, if you bring me to her I love," said Charles.

"Listen to me, prince, I implore you!" cried Bristol, earnestly. "Do not despise my counsels, or you will repent it."

At this moment Buckingham approached the prince on the other side, and whispered in his ear "Go!"

"I mean to do so," replied Charles, in the same tone. "Rise, my good lord," he added to Bristol. "I know that your advice is well meant, but I cannot follow it. You make no allowance for a lover's impatience. An opportunity presents itself to me of seeing the Infanta—think you I will neglect it?"

"My lord of Buckingham, I must appeal to you for aid," said Bristol, earnestly. "The prince has been entrusted to your charge by your sovereign aster. You have the greatest influence with his ghness. Exert it now, and prevent this rash step."

"I am not disposed to regard the matter in the me serious light as yourself, my lord," replied uckingham, indifferently. "Besides, the prince a knight-errant."

"You will be answerable for any ill consequences iat may ensue," said Bristol, sternly.

"I am content to bear the responsibility," re- irned Buckingham, throwing himself with an air great nonchalance into a chair.

"Good night, my lords," cried Charles. "We iall meet early in the morning."

"Long ere that, I trust," said Bristol. "Think ot I shall retire to rest till I know that your high- ess has safely returned."

"I am perfectly easy," laughed Buckingham. I know that Gondomar will take good care of our highness, and I shall, therefore, go to bed s soon as I have supped. Buena fortuna!"

Charles and Gondomar then prepared to qui the room, but Bristol stopped them.

"Hold a moment!" he cried. "Since your high ness is resolved to go in spite of my remonstrances I pray you to leave the house privately, so tha none may know of your departure. I will mak some excuse to your attendants, and give them t understand you have retired to rest. It is of th last consequence that your visit to the palace b kept secret."

"There your lordship is perfectly right," said Gondomar. "Every precaution should be taken to ensure secresy. The visit must not even be suspected."

"To guard against that risk," said Bristol, "do you, count, pass forth as is your wont, and when you are out of the house repair to the garden gate, where I will bring his highness presently. You know the place?"

"Perfectly," replied Gondomar.

And with a significant glance at Buckingham e quitted the room.

As soon as he was gone, the Earl of Bristol pened a window which communicated by a short ight of steps with the garden. Descending by ıis outlet, the prince gained a broad gravel walk, ordered by a parterre, adorned with oleanders, ıyrtles, and other flowering and fragrant shrubs. 'he garden was of considerable extent, and apeared to be charmingly laid out in the formal ıste of the period, with clipped alleys and beds f flowers, and boasted some tall cypresses, and two xtraordinarily large mulberry-trees, which are ven now in existence. The night was calm, the ars shone brightly in the deep blue heavens, the ıoon was in her first quarter, and hung like a cresənt on high. All was hushed in repose, and the lence was only broken by the nightingales amid ıe trees. Viewed from the garden, whence its full ze could be discerned, the mansion presented a əry imposing appearance.

"You are well lodged here, my lord," said Charles, looking back at the house.

"I have no cause for complaint," said Bristol. "There is a good garden, as you see; and though the House of Seven Chimneys is not so large as York House," he added to Buckingham, who had come out with them, "it is large enough for me."

"Are there seven chimneys, my lord?" cried Buckingham. "I doubt it, for I have counted them."

"Most certainly there are," replied Bristol. "It is no misnomer. I will convince you of the fact to-morrow. Your lordship is not the only person puzzled by it. Originally there were only six chimneys, but a seventh was built in jest."

"Under what circumstances?" demanded Charles.

"Your highness shall hear when you have leisure to listen to the story," replied Bristol. "We are now at the gate."

With this, he unlocked the door. Posted on the other side of it they found Gondomar.

"Your highness can come forth," said the latter. 'The coast is quite clear."

"Take the key with you," said Bristol, delivering it to the prince. "Return this way. I will be on the watch for you. I shall not know a moment's peace till I behold you again. Heaven guard your highness!"

Charles then passed out, and having secured the door, accompanied Gondomar along a narrow lane running between high walls, the outer of which skirted the convent of San Geronimo.

On reaching the plazuela, in front of the House of Seven Chimneys, they found Gondomar's coach, and, immediately entering it, were driven along the Calle de Alcala and the Calle Mayor, to the grand plaza in which stood the royal palace.

II.

OF THE MEETING BETWEEN CHARLES AND THE INFANTA MARIA.

The old Palacio Real of Madrid, to which our story refers, must not be confounded with the existing palace, which, comparatively speaking, is a modern building, being only completed about a hundred years ago. The ancient structure was, in fact, the Moorish Alcazar, and had been the abode of the Caliphs till they were driven from New Castile to Granada. It was first occupied as a palace by Enrique IV., towards the close of the fifteenth century, but few changes were made in it till the time of Charles V., when the pile was artially rebuilt and enlarged, and its original cha-acter materially destroyed. Philip II. may be said o be the first Christian monarch who dwelt within he Alcazar of Madrid, for until the completion of he Escorial, in 1584, he made it his chief resi-lence. Not till the reign of this gloomy monarch lid Madrid itself become the capital of Spain, and rom the same epoch must be dated the importance f the city. Few changes were made in the Alcazar y Philip III., who was perfectly content with the alace bequeathed to him by his illustrious sire; nd Philip IV. had as yet been too short a time on he throne to attempt any improvements. Though eterogeneous in its architecture, and certainly not o beautiful as it had been in the days of its Mos-em rulers, the royal palace of Madrid was a vast nd magnificent pile, occupying a most command-ng position on the heights overlooking the valley f the Manzanares. Immediately beneath the royal edifice, extending from the foot of the eminence on which it stood to the banks of the river, was the Campo del Moro, part of which was laid out as gardens.

Viewed either from the grand plaza, from the valley, or from afar, the palace presented a most striking and picturesque appearance. It was entered by two Moorish gates, the beautiful architecture of which was happily undisfigured, and the buildings surrounding the spacious court were studded with cupolas and minarets. Above these towered the ancient keep, with its zig-zag battlements and turrets at each angle. Besides a number of small courts, the palace comprehended a superb patio, surrounded by apartments, laid out in the Arabian style. Such were the principal features of the Alcazar, as it was still generally called. Opportunities of examining it more in detail will occur as we proceed.

The coach of the Conde Gondomar was instantly admitted into the outer court of the palace by the ırders stationed at the gate. In this court several rriages were drawn up, and the place was crowded ith lacqueys in magnificent liveries, grooms of the ıble, arquebusiers, alabarderos, and footmen hold-g torches that cast a ruddy glare on the walls. n alighting, Gondomar and the prince entered the ılace by the grand portal, in front of which a ıard was stationed; but instead of mounting the :and staircase, they passed through a door at the ːar of the spacious vestibule. Charles now found mself in a long passage, dimly lighted by lamps ıng at distant intervals. Evidently communi-ting with the apartments of the various subor-nate officers of the royal household, this passage 'ought them to a back staircase, mounting which, ıey came to an upper corridor, containing the dgings of the meninos, or pages, appointed to tend upon the queen and the Infanta. This cor-dor was lighted in the same manner as that on ıe ground floor, and as Gondomar traversed it, he counted the doors on the right hand, and stopping at the ninth, opened it. The room was vacant, but a lamp was burning on the table, and the noise caused by their entrance brought out from the inner room a tall, handsome young man, attired in a doublet and mantle of orange-coloured satin, embroidered with gold. The menino—for such he was—expressed his surprise by his looks, but he made no remark.

"I want you to do me a service, Pepe," said Gondomar.

"Your lordship has only to command me," replied the menino, bowing.

"It is a very simple matter, and will give you no trouble," said Gondomar. "All I wish you to do is to lend this caballero a dress."

"With the greatest pleasure," returned Pepe. "Pray step this way, señor, and you shall choose one for yourself."

"Hold a moment, Pepe," said Gondomar. "You

ought to understand that the caballero means to personate you."

"Personate me!" exclaimed Pepe, in alarm. "That is quite another affair. Your lordship must excuse me. I don't like it. I shall have to bear the blame of any indiscretion the caballero may commit."

"Give yourself no uneasiness, Pepe," said Gondomar. "The caballero has the strongest motives for caution. Equip him in your newest suit. You shall have it back in an hour."

"In spite of these assurances, my mind misgives me," said Pepe. "But I am under too many obligations to your lordship to refuse. Come with me, señor."

And he took Charles into the inner room, from which, in a short space of time, the prince emerged, attired in garments of orange-coloured satin, like the menino. The habiliments might have been made for him, so well did they fit.

"Bravo! This will do admirably!" cried Gondomar, on beholding him.

"Yes, the caballero makes a very handsome page," said Pepe; "but let him keep clear of the other meninos and ushers, or he will assuredly be detected."

"Never fear," rejoined Gondomar. "Await our return."

So saying, he quitted the room with Charles.

From the corridor the count and the newly-made page proceeded through a variety of passages, up and down staircases, until they came to a superb suite of rooms, the windows of which, Gondomar informed his companion, overlooked the valley of the Manzanares. All these were lighted up, but there was no company within them, only a few attendants standing near the open doors, who bowed respectfully as Gondomar passed on.

At length the count and his companion came to a grand saloon, at the door of which two gentlemen ushers, bearing wands, were stationed. Only the central chandelier was lighted, so that the two extremities of the vast hall were, comparatively speaking, buried in gloom. A concert was going forward in this part of the saloon, and Charles learnt from his conductor that the chief performers at it were members of the royal family. Surrounded by meninos and meninas, intermingled with a few courtiers and ladies of rank, all standing, sat, near a table on which some musical instruments were placed, the young King of Spain, with his youthful and lovely queen, his two brothers, the Infantes Don Carlos and the Cardinal Don Fernando, both of whom were mere boys, and the peerless damsel, whom Charles had travelled so far to behold—the Infanta Maria. There she sat in the midst of the group, the object towards which all eyes were turned, for she had just taken up a mandoline, and was about to sing.

Gondomar and Charles, who had noiselessly advanced to a short distance within the saloon, stood still, and the prince, who was enraptured at the sight of the Infanta, held his breath to listen.

After a brief prelude she began. Her song was one of those romantic ballads which breathe of love and chivalry, and told how a Spanish maiden was carried off by a Moor, and after long captivity was delivered by her knightly lover. The utmost effect possible was given to the words, and Charles was alternately melted by tenderness, moved to pity, and roused to martial enthusiasm. The singer's voice was exquisite, and the prince felt a void in his breast when the sweet notes ceased. Perhaps if she had known whose ears were drinking in those melodious sounds, she could not have produced them.

This ballad closed the concert, and when it was over the royal party fell into conversation. Counselling the prince to remain where he was, Gondomar stepped forward, and, after making a re-

ence to the king and queen, entered into con-
'sation with the Infanta.

Charles was now able to study the features of
mistress, and as he looked at her his admira-
n increased. The Infanta Maria was just seven-
n, and her charms were well calculated to in-
me the prince. She possessed the same slight
nmetrical figure as her sister, Anne of Austria,
d if they had been together it would have been
fficult to decide which of the two was the most
autiful. Maria had tender blue eyes, soft and
ep as summer skies, beautifully pencilled eye-
ows, a ravishingly fair complexion, full lips that
ushed like coral, and teeth like pearls. Her face
as oval in form, and her features charming,
ough not classically moulded. Her tresses were
'a light golden hue. Their sole ornament on the
'esent occasion was an oleander flower, placed at
e side of the head. Her attire was of black
elvet, embroidered with gold, which set off the

dazzling fairness of her skin. Lovely as she was, it was evident that in another year she would be lovelier still. Her manner was graceful and captivating, and had none of the coldness and reserve that Charles expected. He forgot that he saw her when she was entirely unrestrained by etiquette.

When Charles could remove his gaze from the Infanta, he turned to the young King of Spain, whose features strongly resembled those of his sister. Philip had a very youthful appearance—indeed, he was under twenty—and this juvenile look was heightened by a slight graceful figure, blonde locks, large blue eyes, a complexion of almost feminine delicacy, and small hands and feet that even an Andalusian dame might have envied. His features were well formed, but his visage was somewhat long, and he had the protruding under lip which marked his line, and proclaimed him a descendant of Charles V. A fair silken moustache ıded his upper lıp, and with a slight pointed ard ın some degree counteıacted the effeminacy his expression. In stature he was tall, and his rson well proportioned, though slender. His ınner was high bred and haughty. His vest-ents were of carnation satın embroidered with ıck silk and gold, and displayed his elegant ;ure to great advantage. Around his neck he ɔre the Toison d'Or, and the cross of Santiago ıs embroidered on his mantle. Naturally in-lent and feeble in character, the young king was tirely governed by his favourite and minister, e Conde-Duque de Olivarez, but he possessed ghly cultivated tastes, and was a great patron of t and letters.

Philip's two brothers, as we have said, were erely boys—the elder, Don Carlos, not being ore than fifteen—but they were well-grown, ell-favoured striplings, and promised to become ıe-looking men. In aspect and manner, the

Infante Don Carlos differed totally from his brothers. His expression was thoughtful, and his countenance was stamped with a gravity far beyond his years. His features were regular, his complexion dark, his eyes large and black, and his hair, which he wore short, of the same hue. His gravity and dark complexion delighted the people, who remarked, when he showed himself among them, "At last we have got a prince of our own colour." Don Carlos had no particular title or post, but, as heir to the throne, ranked as second person in the kingdom. He had a large revenue, and was allowed precisely the same wardrobe as the king. His costume on the present occasion was of carnation satin, embroidered like that of his royal brother.

The Infante Don Fernando was fair, with blonde locks, tender blue eyes, and a skin soft and smooth as that of a girl. Indeed, with his slim figure and regular features, he looked like a damsel habited s a page. His habiliments were of black velvet. Young as he was, the Infante Don Fernando was prince of the Church, having already acquired he dignity of cardinal. He was also Archbishop f Toledo, accounted the highest spiritual dignity n Christendom after the Papacy, inasmuch as the Chancellorship of Castile was annexed to it, and e possessed the large annual revenue of three undred thousand crowns. At the moment when Charles's eye fell upon him, the boy-cardinal, archishop, and chancellor, who had infinitely more he air of a page than of a grave ecclesiastical ignitary, was conversing with the Papal Nuncio, who formed one of the party, and occupied a seat etween him and the king.

One person alone remains to be described — erhaps the most attractive of the party. This vas the young queen, Elizabeth of France. She vas only just nineteen, and consequently still in he spring of her beauty. But she was very lovely, and had a noble figure. Her transparently white skin set off to perfection her splendid black eyes, arched brows, and rich black tresses. The young queen had great vivacity of manner, laughed frequently so as to display her pearly teeth, and her looks and gestures were so eloquent and expressive that Charles almost fancied he could understand what she said.

Not much time, however, was allowed him for further observation, for it soon became evident that the party was about to break up. The Nuncio was the first to rise. Respectfully saluting their majesties, he retired, being conducted to the side-door by the mayor-domo mayor, the Conde de Puebla. Shortly afterwards the king and queen prepared to depart, and, while taking leave of the Infanta, her majesty embraced her tenderly. The royal pair, followed by the two young princes, and a crowd of courtiers and attendants, and preceded by the Conde de Puebla, passed out at the side-door.

The only person now left of the royal party was the Infanta, and she lingered because Gondomar had made her understand that he had some intelligence to communicate to her.

"What have you to say to me, count?" she whispered, as the attention of the meninos and damsels of honour was diverted by the departure of their majesties.

"Prepare yourself for a great surprise, princesa," replied Gondomar, in the same tone. "He is here."

"He!—who?" exclaimed the Infanta, fixing her large eyes inquiringly upon him.

"Who else could it be but your lover, Don Carlos Estuardo?" replied Gondomar.

"You amaze me!" she cried, blushing deeply. "I did not know the prince was in Madrid."

"He has only just arrived, and no one will be made aware of the circumstance till to-morrow," replied Gondomar. "But he could not control his impatience to behold you, so I consented to bring him here, and make you acquainted with his presence."

"Where—where is he?" demanded the Infanta, in a voice tremulous with emotion, and scarcely daring to look round.

"Yonder—on the right—disguised as a page."

"Heavens! if he should be discovered!" cried the Infanta, with increasing emotion.

"Calm yourself, princesa, or you will attract attention. He is dying to say a word to you."

"It must not be," she replied. "He is imprudent to venture here at all. You should not have brought him, count."

"I could not resist his passionate prayers," said Gondomar. "Neither would you blame me, if you had heard him. Have you not a word for him, princesa?"

"I know not what to say. Tell him—say I bid him welcome."

"Is that all? It is but little, methinks, for a lover who has come so far to behold his mistress."

"No more, my lord. We shall be observed."

On this, Gondomar bowed and fell back, but he ept his eye fixed upon the Infanta.

For a moment she looked irresolute. She then alled to her dueña, Doña Elvira de Medanilla, a ately, middle-aged dame with a severe aspect, ho had luckily been engaged with Padre Amrosio, the Infanta's confessor, during the foregoing iscourse, and signified her intention of retiring. his was the signal for the meninos and meninas to ithdraw, and they accordingly made their reerences to the Infanta, and departed—the pages rooping off in one direction, and the maids of onour in another.

As soon as they were gone, the Infanta made a racious movement to Gondomar, and moved slowly lown the grand saloon, attended by Doña Elvira. Chey passed close by Charles, who bowed reverenially as they drew near.

Then for the first time the eyes of the lovers net, and it was only by a great effort that Charles repressed the impulse that prompted him to spring forward and throw himself at the Infanta's feet. He was still watching her departing figure, as she glided down the saloon, when he was joined by Gondomar.

"What think you of your mistress, prince?" inquired the count

"She is an adorable creature," replied Charles. "Oh! that I could have said one word to her! To be so near and yet be debarred from speech—'tis enough to drive one mad! But look!" he added, with an irrepressible exclamation of delight. "She returns—and alone."

"Nothing like a woman's wit," said Gondomar. "She has contrived to give her dueña the slip, and will afford your highness the opportunity you so eagerly desire of exchanging a word with her."

As they spoke, the Infanta, who had left Doña Elvira at the lower end of the salon, came on quickly. Gondomar, followed by Charles, advanced to meet her.

"I have forgotten my fan, count," said the In-nta, as she approached. "I must have left it on ie table with the music."

"I will bring it to you in an instant, princesa," ied Gondomar, flying towards the table.

The eagerly-desired moment had come. Charles as alone with the Infanta. But his agitation was great that he could scarcely profit by the oppor-inity.

"Forgive me for thus presenting myself before ou, princess," he cried, at length. "Love has rought me to Madrid—love for you, princess. ove, therefore, must plead my excuse. Your nage cheered me on during my long and toilsome urney, and when I arrived here this evening, I as determined, at all hazards, to behold you. I ave, therefore, presented myself to you in this uise. Forgive me, princess! forgive me!"

"You plead so earnestly, prince, that I must rgive you," she replied. "I ought not to have ranted this interview—so contrary to etiquette and propriety. But I could not allow you to go away without telling you how sensible I am of your gallantry and devotion."

"Oh, princess!" exclaimed Charles, passionately. "I dare not throw myself at your feet and tell you how much I adore you. But I implore you to satisfy me that my love is not unrequited."

"I think I can love you, prince," she rejoined. "But I must consult others before I dare answer the question explicitly."

"What others?" cried Charles. "In such a case you have only to consult your own heart."

"But I have been taught that in trusting to such guidance I may be misled," replied the Infanta. "My feelings may deceive me."

"Say not so, princess!" cried Charles. "The heart never deceives. It will not be tutored. Speak, then, according to its dictates, and answer me frankly—can you love me?"

"I am forbidden—strictly forbidden—to answer

ıch a question, prince, without the king, my bro-ıer's, consent," she replied.

"Who has forbidden you?" demanded Charles.

"My confessor, Padre Ambrosio—my dueña, oña Elvira—all who have charge of me," re-rned the Infanta.

"Have they ever spoken to you of me?" asked harles.

"Often. They are constantly talking about you. hey describe you as a charming young prince, ıt——"

"But what?" cried Charles. "Do not hesitate tell me."

"They say you have one great fault, which ıunterbalances all your merits. You are a he-tic."

"Why, so I am in religion, but not in love, veetest Maria," returned Charles, smiling. "But mean to allow you the free exercise of your faith. 'ill not that suffice? It ought, methinks."

"It would be far better if you could conform to my faith," said the Infanta. "There would then be no obstacle to our union, and I should feel that it would be approved by Heaven. You would then be without a fault, and I could give you my entire affection."

"And can you not give it me as it is?" demanded Charles.

"I cannot promise," she rejoined. "I must first try to convert you."

"The effort will be vain, princess," said Charles. "My religious tenets are unchangeable But I promise you — and indeed the king my father has solemnly engaged for me—that you shall have the full and free exercise of your own faith—you and your children. That is all I can do. Is it not enough?"

"I must consider," replied the Infanta. "I must consult Padre Ambrosio."

"I feel I have an enemy in your confessor,

incess," said Charles. "But I did not anticipate discussion like this on our first meeting."

"It is best we should understand each other, ince," she returned. "I am a devout Catholic."

"You are a bigot, but a very charming one, aria," said Charles.

At this moment Gondomar returned.

"Your fan, princesa," he said, bowing and de- ering it to her.

"You have been long, count," she remarked, ith a smile.

"Nay, madam, I feared to interrupt."

"Adios, prince," cried the Infanta to Charles. Think of what I have said to you."

"One word more before we part, Maria?" he ied.

She made no response, but tripped off to her ieña.

"All has gone well, I trust, prince?" inquired ondomar.

"The Infanta is charming, but somewhat bigoted," returned Charles. "She has told me plainly that she will convert me, and I have told her equally plainly that she will fail in the attempt."

"This is the work of her confessor, Padre Ambrosio, who has enjoined her to make your highness's adoption of the faith of Rome the price of her hand," said Gondomar. "But rest easy. The king will give her to you without any conditions. But now that our object has been attained, the sooner we depart the better."

They then quitted the saloon. In the antechamber through which they had to pass several courtiers were collected, and Gondomar was obliged to stop for a moment to speak to them. Charles moved on to a short distance, and waited for him.

As soon as Gondomar could disengage himself, he was hurrying towards the prince, when a tall, handsome young man, attired in murrey-coloured

ret, and possessing a very striking physiog-
ny, stopped him.

"A moment, count," said the young man.
blige me with the name of yonder page. It is
first time I have seen him in the palace. He
a very remarkable countenance, and a very
ely figure. I should like to paint him."

"I will tell him so," replied Gondomar. "He
be proud to hear that he has attracted the
ntion of so great a painter as Don Diego Velas-
z de Silva."

But you do not tell me his name, count," said
asquez.

You shall know it to-morrow, Don Diego,"
rned Gondomar, hastily.

Meantime, I will tell it you," rejoined Velas-
:. "I noticed him in the grand salon just now,
I then suspected who he was, though, as he
aloof, I could not be quite sure. But now I
no doubt whatever on the point. There can-

not be two such heads. That page, my lord, i Prince Charles of England."

"Hush!" exclaimed Gondomar. "Let your lip be fast sealed, Don Diego."

"Fear not, my lord," said Velasquez. "Th prince's secret is safe with me. I dare not mak the request, but if his highness will deign to sit t me for his portrait, he will confer the greates obligation upon me."

"I will not fail to mention the matter to him Don Diego," replied Gondomar. "Meantime, rely on your secresy."

With this he bowed to Velasquez, and re joining Charles, told him what had just occurred mentioning, at the same time, the request of th great painter.

"It will gratify him deeply if your highnes thinks fit to comply with it," he said.

"He shall paint my portrait for the Infanta, a a companion picture to the one painted by him o ıer highness, which is in my possession," rejoined Charles. "Tell him so."

"I will make him happy at once," replied Gon-.omar.

And he flew back to Velasquez, whose dark heek flushed, and whose eyes brightened, as the ıessage was communicated to him. Placing his .and upon his heart with a look of ineffable grati-ude, he bowed to the prince, who graciously re-urned the salute.

All this passed with great rapidity, and fortu-ately did not attract attention.

In another minute Charles and Gondomar were raversing corridors and passages, making their way owards Pepe's lodging, which they reached with-ut further interruption. Here the prince resumed is own attire with as much expedition as possible, nd having warmly thanked the menino for the ervice he had rendered him, he proceeded with

Gondomar to the great court, where they found the coach waiting for them.

Ere long they had reached the House of Seven Chimneys, and alighting in the plazuela, at once repaired to the garden gate. On unlocking it, they found the Earl of Bristol, who was keeping watch, wrapped in his cloak.

Gondomar then took his leave, promising to make his appearance at an early hour on the morrow, to receive the prince's commands.

"Heaven be praised your highness has got back in safety!" exclaimed Bristol. "Have you seen the Infanta?"

"Seen her and spoken with her," replied Charles.

"Amazement!" cried the earl. "This is indeed a romantic incident."

"You will say so, my lord, when you learn all particulars," replied the prince.

Having secured the gate, the earl conducted the

ince to the house. All the inmates had retired rest, but a collation was laid out in one of the ver rooms. Charles, however, declined to partake it, and was at once taken to the spacious cham- r prepared for him. A magnificent couch invited n to repose, and shortly afterwards, throwing nself upon it, he sunk into slumber.

III.

THE WHITE DOVE.

The windows of the chamber in which Charles slept looked towards the garden, and as he arose, perfectly refreshed by a night of sound repose, he attired himself without waiting for his attendants, and threw open the casement. The morning was bright and beautiful, the sky cloudless and of the deepest blue, and a gentle breeze came laden with the scent of orange-blossoms and fragrant flowers.

Beyond the garden walls, on the left, arose the roof of the convent of San Francisco, with a church adjoining it, the bells of which were now jingling musically. On the right, through an opening amid the houses, could be seen in the distance the lofty range of the Guadarrama mountains, with their jagged peaks covered with snow. The garden itself, with its orange-groves, its tall cypresses, its two large mulberry-trees, each with a seat beneath it, its parterres and pleasant walks, adorned with statues and marble urns filled with flowers, seemed to invite him to stroll forth.

A charming concert arose from the trees, and Charles was listening to the melodious strains poured forth by the little warblers, when a snow-white dove, which had been gently cooing in one of the mulberry-trees, flew towards the casement at which he stood, and, without manifesting the slightest alarm, alighted on the sill close beside him. Charles did not move, for fear of disturbing the bird, and there it remained pluming itself and regarding him with its lovely eyes, until the opening of the chamber door scared it away. Greatly to Charles's satisfaction, however, the dove almost instantly returned, and settled on the same spot. The person who had just entered the chamber was Sir Richard Graham, and the prince pointed out his pretty visitor to him.

"The appearance of this beautiful bird, the emblem of all that is pure and holy, at a juncture like the present, may be accepted as a fortunate omen," said Charles. "Do you not think so, Sir Richard?"

"Assuredly, your highness," replied Graham. "But to my mind the dove looks like a love-messenger, and may have a letter from the Infanta under its wing."

"Poh! that is an idle thought," replied Charles. "The poor bird brings me no letter, but it gives me hope."

"A propos of letters, I have one for your highness," remarked Graham.

"From the king my father?" cried Charles, eagerly.

"No," replied Graham. "You will be surprised vhen you learn from whom it comes. I pray your ighness to observe the superscription—'Al muy oble, y muy ilustre Señor, Don Carlos Estuardo.'"

"Who can have written it?" cried Charles, in urprise.

"You can satisfy your curiosity by breaking the eal," said Graham. "But, before doing so, let ne offer you an agreeable piece of information. The two barbs given you by the Duke de Cea ave been sent back."

"Indeed!" exclaimed the prince.

"They were brought here by two muleteers efore daylight this morning," said Graham, "and re now safe in the stables of the House of Seven Chimneys. Perhaps that letter may relate to hem."

"Prithee, read it to me," said Charles.

Graham then opened the letter, and read aloud s follows:

"SERENISIMO SEÑOR!

"Though a robber, I am a man of honour.

"Your highness will, therefore, conceive how deep must have been my displeasure on finding that two of my band, Melchior and Geronimo, had dared to carry off the horses which your highness and the noble marquis accompanying you had condescended to take in exchange for your barbs.

"In order to meet the justice of the case, and as an example to their comrades, I immediately caused both rascals to be shot. I trust their punishment will be satisfactory to your highness.

"But, after an occurrence so opposed to my notions of honourable conduct, I cannot think of retaining the barbs, and I therefore send them back to your highness and the noble marquis, with a profound expression of regret for the annoyance you have experienced.

"Your highness will not be surprised that I am acquainted with your exalted rank, as well as with the rank of your noble companion, when I inform you that a courier from London, bearing despatches from your royal father, and two couriers from Paris, with despatches mentioning your visit to that capital, are now in my hands. These couriers shall remain for twelve hours in the Somosierra, as I have reason to believe their detention for that time will be agreeable to your highness. They shall then come on with the despatches.

"Your highness, I trust, will credit me when I state that, had I been aware at the time whom I had the honour of escorting, you should never have known me as other than Capitan Mendez.

"Viva le Principe de Inglaterra!

"EL CORTEJO."

"A strange epistle!" exclaimed Charles, laughing. "This fellow piques himself upon his nice sense of honour. He richly deserves it, no doubt, but I should be sorry to see him hanged."

"He deserves to be rewarded rather than hanged," rejoined Graham. "He has made all the amends in his power by shooting those two rascals and sending back the barbs. In fact, he has rendered your highness an important service. Had he not detained the couriers, your arrival in Madrid must have been known last night, and then you could not have taken the king and Olivarez by surprise."

"Nor have visited the palace last night," said Charles, smiling.

"Is it possible you did so?" cried Graham, in amazement. "I thought your highness had retired to rest early."

"I spent more than an hour at the palace, and saw the whole of the royal family in their privacy."

"Without making yourself known?"

"Without making myself known—save to the Infanta."

"By Heaven! you have done wonders!" exlaimed Graham. "The Duke de Cea spoke of he strictness of Spanish court etiquette, and delared it would be impossible for your highness to btain a private interview with the Infanta."

"De Cea was wrong, Dick. The impossibility ıas already been accomplished," replied Charles, ıughing.

"In truth, your highness is a veritable preux hevalier, and has come to conquer," said Graham. 'The affair is already settled."

"Not quite," rejoined Charles, gravely. "I hould have felt rather despondent this morning, ıad not that dove cheered me."

Just at this moment the door was opened by 3uckingham, who unceremoniously entered, ac:ompanied by Gondomar. The marquis was arrayed n the splendid habiliments which he had procured rom Marolles in Paris.

"I have to congratulate your highness on your

success last night," he said. "You have begun the game admirably, and have won the first stake. Gondomar tells me you have not only seen the Infanta, but conversed with her."

"I owe my success entirely to the count's management," said Charles. "But on calm reflection I feel it was a very rash proceeding, and ought not to have been undertaken."

"Repentance comes too late," said Buckingham. "But I see nothing to regret."

"Having just come from the palace," said Gondomar, "I am able to give your highness positive assurance that your secret visit is wholly unsuspected. In fact, no rumour whatever of your arrival at Madrid has as yet got abroad. I have come here to learn your pleasure, but as certain formalities must be observed, I will venture to suggest that my lord of Buckingham shall accompany me to acquaint his majesty with your arrival."

"Precisely the course I meant to enjoin," said

Charles. "Go at once. I will not stir forth till you return. Yet stay!" he added, arresting their departure. "It may be proper to consult my lord of Bristol before you take this step."

"I cannot consult Bristol on any point," said Buckingham, haughtily. "If your highness thinks fit, let him go with Gondomar. But in that case they must go without me."

"Nay, in Heaven's name, go!" said Charles, who was well aware of the jealous nature of his favourite.

Buckingham and Gondomar then bowed and withdrew, and as the door closed upon them, Charles muttered to himself, "Henceforward I shall be a mere puppet in the hands of others—to be played with as they think proper."

Shortly afterwards, the prince took a solitary stroll in the garden to enjoy the beauty of the morning, and think over his interview with the Infanta. With mixed emotions, he recalled each word she had uttered, and, in spite of all his efforts to shake it off, a fear came over him that his hopes would be blighted. To lose the Infanta would be worse than death. Yet it was possible, from what she had said, that religious differences might separate them.

While indulging in these meditations, he had seated himself beneath one of the mulberry-trees. A slight noise attracted his attention, and looking up, he perceived that the milk-white dove had settled over his head.

"That gentle bird gives me new hope," he ejaculated. "I will cast off all doubt and despondency. The Infanta will be mine."

End of the Second Book.

BOOK III.

THE CONDE-DUQUE DE OLIVAREZ.

I.

HOW BUCKINGHAM WAS PRESENTED TO OLIVAREZ.

BUCKINGHAM and Gondomar, entering the coach of the latter, drove to the palace of the Conde-Duque de Olivarez, a noble edifice, charmingly situated at the northern extremity of the Calle de Alcala, on the brow of the eminence overlooking the woody valley of the Prado.

The internal arrangements of the mansion corresponded with its superb exterior. Excepting the royal palace, no other princely residence in Madrid possessed such a splendid suite of apartments as the palace of the Conde-Duque. On the side of the

Prado was a broad terrace forming a delightful promenade, and communicating with the vast garden at the rear of the noble pile. The grand façade of the palace looked towards the Calle de Alcala, from which it was separated by a broad and well-paved court, defended by a gilt railing. In the centre of the railing was a lofty iron gateway, very elaborately and beautifully wrought, and embellished with the armorial bearings of the ancient and illustrious house of Guzman.

As Buckingham drove through this gateway, and contemplated the imposing façade, he could not help acknowledging that it was an abode worthy of a great minister—but the splendour of the palace increased his desire to lower the pride of its owner. Buckingham hated Olivarez because he possessed the same sort of influence over Philip IV. that he himself had over James I. He looked upon the Spanish minister as a rival and an enemy, whose humiliation would heighten his own glory.

At the period of which we write, the three most important kingdoms in Europe were governed by favourites, supreme and almost irresponsible power being confided to them by their respective sovereigns. Thus the destinies of France were committed to Richelieu—those of Spain to Olivarez—those of England to Buckingham. By far the ablest and most sagacious of the three was Richelieu, and not without reason he despised his rivals. Still they were formidable from the power they possessed, and, united, might have crushed him. But the mutual distrust entertained of each other by Buckingham and Olivarez prevented any such alliance. There was no league possible between two ministers, each of whom believed that the other was playing false. With this insight into Buckingham's breast, it will easily be understood with what feelings he regarded his approaching meeting with his rival.

But before describing that meeting, let us say a word as to the powerful Spanish minister.

Don Gaspar Guzman, Conde-Duque de Olivarez, had risen to his present eminent position, when Philip IV., at that time too young to undertake the charge of government, ascended the throne. Before that period, by attaching himself zealously to the youthful prince, Olivarez had succeeded in obtaining unbounded influence over him. Consequently, on Philip's accession to power his own elevation was certain. His ascendancy over the feeble monarch was absolute, and Philip, without an effort, resigned himself to the sway of his favourite.

Olivarez had many qualities that well fitted him for the important post he occupied—great capacity for business, unwearied application, shrewdness, and caution. But he was arrogant, vindictive, and unrelenting, and his harshness made him numerous enemies. Perfidious himself, he was distrustful of others. His leading idea was to give a preponderating influence in Europe to the House of

Austria, and he thought that the marriage of the Infanta with the heir to the throne of England would further his designs, but suspicious of James and Buckingham, he was resolved not to permit the completion of the match till he had secured solid advantages for Spain, and with this view he protracted the negotiation on one pretext or another, constantly making a fresh demand when any point had been conceded. Disgusted by his perpetual subterfuges, Bristol was more than once on the point of breaking off the treaty; but this was not what Olivarez desired, and by promises and professions, never meant to be fulfilled, he succeeded in cajoling the English ambassador.

Olivarez was now in the very prime of life, being between thirty and forty. He possessed a countenance of great shrewdness and intelligence lighted up by large penetrating black eyes, which seemed to emit flashes of fire when he was animated or angry. His complexion was exceedingly dark; his features regular and handsome. He was of middle height, and well formed. In manner he was a thorough Castilian, cold, reserved, and exceedingly haughty, but his arrogance could be laid aside if needful.

Such was Don Gaspar de Guzman, Conde-Duque de Olivarez, chief Cupbearer to the king, Grand Master of the Horse, chief of the Council of State, and prime minister.

The aim of Olivarez was to surpass the Duke of Lerma in splendour, so he kept up a princely retinue, and gave magnificent entertainments. Like his royal master, he was a great patron of the arts, and had a splendid gallery of pictures, to which he was constantly making large additions.

The Countess de Olivarez, who was some ten years younger than her lord, and sprung from an illustrious Andalusian family, possessed all the beauty and witchery of a daughter of that sunny region, and was esteemed one of the loveliest and sprightliest dames of the court. The gallants averred that the Conde-Duque was foolish enough to be jealous of his charming spouse, but they did not venture to add that she gave him cause for jealousy.

Though Olivarez had spies at the court of Whitehall, who gave him early information of every matter of moment, yet, owing to the precautions taken by James in closing the ports, no intelligence of the prince's journey had reached him, and being totally ignorant of the arrival of the travellers in Madrid, he was quite unprepared for Buckingham's visit.

He was standing at the time with the countess on a broad marble balcony overlooking the valley of the Prado, his gaze wandering over the woody valley from the ancient monasterio de Atocha to the Puerta de Recoletos, midway between which his palace was situated, when an usher announced the Conde de Gondomar.

"His lordship is not alone," continued the usher. "There is a caballero with him, whom he did not name, but who looks like a person of distinction."

"Did the count request a private audience, Juan?" asked Olivarez.

"No, my lord," returned the usher. "I think he merely desires to present to your excellency the caballero I have mentioned, who appears to be a stranger."

"I will come to them instantly," said the Conde-Duque.

The usher bowed and retired.

"Come with me, madam," said Olivarez to the countess. "Gondomar may desire to present this stranger to you."

They then passed through the open casement into a large and splendidly-furnished apartment, at the farther end of which stood Gondomar and Buckingham.

The tall and stately figure of Buckingham at

once caught the eye of Olivarez, and though he was far from suspecting the truth, he felt certain that the stranger was no ordinary individual.

"What a noble-looking person!" exclaimed the duchess, who was equally struck by Buckingham's appearance. "Who can he be?"

"We shall learn that soon enough," rejoined the Conde-Duque, somewhat sharply. "Something warns me he is an enemy."

"Poh! your excellency is always suspicious," said the duchess.

On his part, Buckingham regarded his rival with equal curiosity.

The Conde-Duque, we may mention, was attired in a doublet and cloak of tawny taffeta, thickly laced with silver. His hat, which he had put on, was fastened at the side by a superb diamond brooch, and adorned with tawny plumes.

The countess, who moved with the incomparable grace of an Andalusian dame, and who had the smallest feet imaginable, and the largest eyes, was dressed in black satin, deeply fringed with black lace; and though the attire was simple, none could have better suited her exquisite figure. Her ebon tresses were draped in a magnificent black lace mantilla, and harmonised well with her rich Southern complexion and splendid black eyes, soft as velvet, and shaded by long silken lashes. In her hand she carried a fan.

"Is that the duchess?" inquired Buckingham, who was greatly struck by her beauty.

Gondomar replied in the affirmative, adding, "She is a charming creature; but do not fall in love with her. Olivarez is as jealous as a Moor"

"I make no promises," replied Buckingham, smiling. "Those eyes are enough to tempt Saint Anthony himself."

Gondomar then moved on, followed by Buckingham, and approaching Olivarez, said, "Permit me to present to your excellency the Lord Marquis of Buckingham, who is newly arrived in Madrid."

Master as he usually was of himself, Olivarez absolutely started with surprise at the announcement.

"What! my lord of Buckingham here!" he exclaimed.

"So this is the Marquis of Buckingham! I felt sure it must be some very important personage!" mentally ejaculated the countess.

"Ay, your excellency," replied Buckingham, bowing. "I have been sent by my royal master, the King of England, to see whether we cannot bring this long protracted marriage-treaty to a happy issue."

"You may account it concluded, since such is your errand, my dear lord," said Olivarez. "This indeed is a joyful surprise. I am delighted to see your lordship, and so, I am sure, will be his majesty."

"Your excellency is most obliging," replied Buckingham, bowing. "But let me entreat you to present me to the countess."

Olivarez instantly complied, and profound salutations were exchanged between them. After a few compliments had passed, Buckingham said, "I think there is a better chance that the match may be speedily concluded, as the Prince of Wales has come in person to claim his bride."

At this unexpected announcement the minister's dark cheek flushed, but he quickly recovered himself, and gave vent to the most extravagant protestations of delight.

"His majesty must be made instantly acquainted with the welcome news of the prince's arrival," he said. "It will gladden him as much as it does me. Your lordship, I trust, will accompany me to the palace, when I will present you to my royal master, and you can make the gladsome tidings known to him with your own lips. Everything shall be done to manifest our sense of the signal honour conferred upon us. After you have seen the king, I will go with you to pay my reverence to the prince."

"The prince must be a model of gallantry to undertake this journey for his mistress," said the countess. "I long to announce his arrival to the Infanta."

"Then come with us to the palace," said the Conde-Duque. "You shall be the first to give her the joyous intelligence."

"Not quite the first," said Gondomar, aside, to Buckingham.

Shortly afterwards a splendid carriage, drawn by four horses, and attended by a mounted escort, was dashing along the Calle de Alcala, in the direction of the royal palace. The large windows of this roomy carriage showed that there were four persons inside it, three of whom were immediately recognised by those who gazed at the gorgeous equipage, but the fourth was a stranger.

II.

PHILIP IV.

On that morning, Philip had given a private audience to the Nuncio, and the Papal envoy was still with the king, when Olivarez, unannounced, entered the royal cabinet. It being quite evident, from the minister's looks, that he had matter of importance to communicate to his majesty, the Nuncio immediately arose and prepared to retire.

"A moment, monseñor," said Olivarez, stopping him; "let me ask whether you have heard further from his Holiness? Will he send the dispensation for the marriage of the Infanta with the Prince of Wales?"

"Not till he receives positive assurance that etter terms will be made with England," replied ıe Nuncio. "The matter rests entirely with your xcellency. His Holiness knows your desire to romote the interests of the Church of Rome, and hen you deem it expedient, the dispensation will e sent—but not till then."

"Enough, monseñor," replied Olivarez, bowing. In all probability it will be soon required."

"I rejoice to hear it, my lord," said the Nuncio, for I infer that you expect to gain your point." And bowing to the minister, he quitted the cainet.

"I am not so sanguine as your excellency apears to be," remarked Philip, as soon as they were lone. "I do not think we shall extort any furher concessions from the King of England."

"It is in your majesty's power to impose upon im any conditions you think proper," said Olivarez.

"How?" exclaimed Philip. "What has changed the aspect of affairs?"

"An act of folly—inconceivable folly—on the part of the British Solomon," returned Olivarez. "What will your majesty say if I tell you that this crafty and suspicious monarch has exhibited a blind confidence scarcely to be looked for in a rash and inexperienced youth?"

"What has he done? Explain yourself, my lord!" cried Philip.

"He has parted with his son—with the heir to the throne—and consigned him to your majesty's care."

"I cannot think you are trifling with me, my lord," said Philip. "Yet what you say sounds like a jest."

"It is scarcely credible, I own, sire; but, nevertheless, it is true that the Prince of Wales is now in Madrid. He arrived here last night, having ridden the whole distance by post, like a courier, tended only by the Marquis of Buckingham and ree other gentlemen, and is now lodged with the arl of Bristol."

"Amazement!" exclaimed the king. "And you id no intelligence of this journey, my lord?—ou, who are usually so well informed."

"The journey appears to have been so suddenly solved upon, and such precautions were taken to eep it secret, that information could not possibly e sent me," replied Olivarez. "For three days ie ports were kept rigorously closed by James, so iat no couriers could overtake the prince, and he id the marquis travelled under feigned names, id speeded on without halt, save for a day at aris."

"By Santiago! a gallant exploit!" cried Philip. Charles Stuart seems to have the spirit of a night errant."

"Whatever spirit he may possess, he has com-iitted a great imprudence," said Olivarez. "It is now for your majesty to consider what course you will pursue in regard to him."

"No consideration is required, my lord. There is but one course to pursue—receive him with open arms," cried Philip. "He has trusted to my loyalty, and shall find he has not misjudged me."

"I do not desire to check your majesty's noble impulses," rejoined Olivarez, "but you must not throw away the extraordinary advantage you have gained. Receive the prince, as you propose, with all cordiality and honour. But his marriage with the Infanta must not take place till his conversion has been effected."

"That, indeed, would be a masterstroke," said Philip, after a moment's reflection. "But do you really think it can be achieved?"

"Nothing so easy, sire, now we have him here. He has been foolish in coming to us, but we should be doubly foolish if we let him go back without gaining our point."

"Such conduct appears to me disloyal and unworthy," said Philip.

"It is perfectly justifiable," rejoined Olivarez. "The prince has not been lured hither by any false promises from your majesty or from me, but has come of his own free will, and must take the consequences of his rashness. I should be unworthy of the post I hold if I did not prescribe a course from which, I trust, your majesty will not swerve. As I have said, let the prince be received with all honour. But he must be virtually a prisoner."

A cloud came over Philip's brow.

"A prisoner! Charles Stuart a prisoner!" he exclaimed. "I disapprove of the plan, my lord."

"Your majesty misapprehends me," said Olivarez. "I do not mean that the prince shall be subjected to any personal restraint. His prison shall be a chamber in this palace, his gaolers shall be your majesty and myself, nor shall he be aware that he is a captive unless he attempts to depart.

He must be detained, on one pretext or another, till such time as we have accomplished our purpose. You must give him all sorts of grand entertainments—fêtes, masques, banquets, tournaments, and bull-fights. But, above all, your majesty must assign him and the marquis apartments in the palace, so that, without appearing to restrain them, you may have them in safe keeping. Our plans can then be put into operation for effecting the prince's conversion, and to this most desirable end the Infanta herself will be an important instrument. And now, having hastily explained my views, I must inform your majesty that the lord marquis is in the ante-chamber, anxiously waiting to be presented to you."

Philip, desiring that Buckingham should be at once admitted, Olivarez left the cabinet, returning the next moment with the marquis and Gondomar.

Buckingham threw himself on his knees before the king, but Philip instantly raised him.

"My first duty is to deliver this letter to your majesty," said the marquis, producing a despatch. "It is from the king my master. In it he recommends the prince his son to your majesty, and explains the motive of his highness's journey."

So saying, with a profound reverence he presented the letter to the king.

"I thank you, my good lord," said Philip. "I will read the letter anon. Had I known of his highness's coming, he should have had a reception worthy of him, and should have been escorted from the frontiers of the kingdom to this city. I myself would have met him at Burgos, attended by all the grandees of my court. Believe me, I am sensibly touched by the gallantry and courage he has displayed. I long to behold him and embrace him, and thank him for the honour he has done me and my sister, the Infanta Maria."

"His highness is equally anxious to behold your majesty," returned Buckingham, "and only awaits your gracious permission to present himself."

"No, no, that must not be," said Philip. "His highness has no suitable equipage—no retinue. He is lodged at the Earl of Bristol's casa, as I understand. I will visit him there."

"Pardon me, sire, if I venture, in his highness's name, to decline the proffered honour," rejoined Buckingham. "The prince would never permit so great a condescension on your part. He feels that he ought first to wait on your majesty."

"But I must insist," cried Philip.

"Nay, sire, if you are resolved, the prince must of course give way," replied Buckingham.

"I will arrange the matter, so that there shall be no violation of etiquette," interposed Olivarez. "Your majesty and the prince shall meet on equal terms. With your permission, sire, I will attend my lord of Buckingham to pay my respects to his highness."

"Go, my lord," replied Philip; "and tell his highness that I am enchanted to hear of his arrival in Madrid, and but for certain forms, would fly to welcome and embrace him. Say all this for me, my lord, and add that I place my palace at his disposal, and that there is nothing he can ask that I will not grant—nothing I will leave undone to gratify and content him. You have heard what I say, my good lord," he added to Buckingham, "and will not fail, I trust, to repeat my words to the prince your master."

Buckingham bowed profoundly.

"Conde de Gondomar," pursued Philip, "it may be agreeable to the Prince of Wales to have your attendance. It is my pleasure, therefore, that you attach yourself to the person of his highness during his stay in Madrid. Assist him with your counsel in all things, as if you were an Englishman."

"It will delight me to obey your majesty," said Gondomar, bowing.

"And now, my lords," said Philip, "I pray you

hasten to the prince, and bid him welcome in my name. Be not niggard in your speech. Aught you may say will fall short of what I desire to convey."

"The prince shall have an exact report of all your gracious expressions, sire," returned Buckingham.

And bowing profoundly, he quitted the cabinet with Olivarez and Gondomar.

III.

PADRE AMBROSIO.

At the same hour, in another apartment of the palace, sat the Infanta, with Doña Elvira de Medanilla and her meninas. The princess was engaged in embroidering a cushion, but did not proceed very sedulously with her task, and her silence and preoccupied manner attracted the notice of her attendants.

It was a relief when the Countess de Olivarez entered the chamber. The countess was a great favourite with the Infanta, and on seeing her,

Maria immediately laid down her embroidery and flew to embrace her.

"What happy chance brings you to the palace so early this morning, countess?" inquired the Infanta.

"I accompanied the Conde-Duque, who has some affairs to transact with his majesty," replied the countess. "But I want to have a word with you in private, princess."

On hearing this, Doña Elvira and the meninas prepared to withdraw.

"I hope your ladyship will be able to extract some conversation from the princess," said Doña Elvira. "She has scarcely opened her lips this morning."

"What has made you so dull, princess?" inquired the countess, as the dueña quitted the room.

"I know not," replied the Infanta, blushing. "I have a slight headache. I did not sleep well last night."

"You did not dream of the prince, your suitor, I suppose?" said the countess.

"How strange you should ask me the question," returned Maria. "Yes, I *did* dream of him. I thought he had come to Madrid on purpose to see me."

"Can she have heard?" mentally exclaimed the countess, surprised. "But no! no! that is impossible. Was that all your dream, princess?" she added, playfully.

"No," replied Maria, "there was a great deal more. I thought the prince obtained admittance to the palace in the disguise of a page."

"Oh! indeed!" exclaimed the countess. "He was disguised as a page, eh? Pray go on, princess. I am deeply interested by your recital. Did the disguised prince speak to you?"

"Of course. I could not let him go without a word, since he had come so far to see me."

"I hope you have not mentioned your dream to any one else, princess?" remarked the countess.

"You must not attempt to deceive me. You have seen your lover. You have spoken with him. I came to inform you of his arrival in Madrid, but I find he has been beforehand with me. Well, I am not surprised at it. Such gallantry was to be expected from a lover so enterprising. But I trust to Heaven the adventure may not be discovered."

"No fear of that," cried the Infanta. "But have you seen the prince, countess?"

"No, but I have seen his favourite, the Marquis of Buckingham, who has accompanied him on the journey, and who is a splendid-looking personage. Is the prince as handsome as you expected?"

"Much handsomer. He has noble features—the finest eyes I ever beheld—and a charming expression of countenance."

"Then you feel that you really *can* love him, eh?"

"I fear that I love him already, and that is what troubles me," returned the Infanta.

"The conviction need give you no uneasiness," ›marked the countess, smiling. "The prince has right to your heart."

"He will have, when we are affianced," replied Iaria. "But that ceremonial cannot take place ntil after his conversion. I told him so last ight."

"You were too hasty. Suppose the prince ıould refuse to change his creed?"

"Then he must go back without me."

"Ah! you will think differently when you have ›en more of him," said the countess. "If he is ›ally as charming as you describe him, you will ever be able to refuse him, even though he should ontinue obstinate in his heresy. Were I in your lace, I should not allow a question of faith to ıterfere with my happiness."

"Listen to me, countess," said the Infanta, "and will open my heart to you. A struggle has long een going on in my breast between my sense of uty and my affections. So much has been said to me of Prince Charles, and the possibility of my marriage with him has been so much discussed, that I could not fail to dwell upon his image, and though I had never seen him, I began to love him. My heart was wholly unoccupied, and his image fixed itself there. I could think of no one else. I gazed upon his picture till I fancied it endowed with life. He haunted my dreams at night. Questioned by my confessor, I explained the state of my feelings to him, and was reproved sharply for my indulgence in such idle fancies, and enjoined to turn away my thoughts from the prince. 'You must never wed him, princess,' said Padre Ambrosio, 'unless he will consent to abjure his heresies and enter into the bosom of our Church. If you do, you will endanger your soul.'"

"But if Pope Gregory XV. sends the dispensation, you may wed the prince without any apprehension," rejoined the countess. "Besides, many marriages are made between Romanists and Protestants without the consent of his Holiness."

"So I remarked to Padre Ambrosio," observed ie Infanta, "but he contends that no princess in so wed without a dispensation; and he affirms iat the Pope is averse to the match, and will ever consent to it unless the prince is converted."

"How comes Padre Ambrosio to be so well in- ormed as to his Holiness's intentions?" asked the ountess.

"The Nuncio has shown him a letter from the ope," replied the Infanta. "Thus, you see, coun- ss, that I am bound to check all my impulses of fection towards the prince. This was an easy isk formerly—but now that I have seen him— ow that I have encountered his ardent gaze—now iat I have listened to his protestations of love— iy feelings are no longer under my control. I love harles Stuart, countess—I love him I dare not onfess so much to Padre Ambrosio; but to you, ho can sympathise with me, I will avow the uth."

"I do sincerely sympathise with you, sweet princess," said the countess, "but I see no reason for anxiety. Had not the prince come to claim you, I believe the match would never have taken place, but now that he is here all difficulties will vanish."

"You really think so, countess?" cried the Infanta, joyfully.

"I do, indeed," she replied, with an earnestness that left no doubt of her sincerity.

"Will you let me talk to you about the prince sometimes?" said the Infanta. "I have no friend—no confidante. I dare not speak to the king my brother—I cannot speak to the queen."

"You shall have a friend and adviser in me, princess, and if you will follow my counsels all will go well, in spite of Padre Ambrosio."

At this moment a side-door opened, and the person alluded to entered the room. Padre Ambrosio was tall, dark, spare in figure, and had a searching look and a stern expression of countenance.

"I see my news has been anticipated, princess," said, glancing at the countess. "I came to tell u that the Prince of Wales has most unexpectedly ived in Madrid."

"Yes, father, the princess has already received joyful intelligence from me," rejoined the counss.

"What interpretation does your ladyship put on his journey?" demanded Padre Ambrosio.

"What other interpretation can I put, except at he has come to fetch his bride?" she anvered.

"That is one motive, doubtless, but not the incipal motive. He would not have come hither this manner unless he designed to become a conrt."

"Oh no, you are mistaken, father," cried the ifanta. "The prince has no such design."

"How know you that, princess? You have not en him—ha?" cried Padre Ambrosio, quickly.

"What a question to ask, father?" interposed the countess. "How can she have seen him?"

"She appears confused," muttered Padre Ambrosio, as he watched the Infanta. "There is some concealment here."

At this moment Doña Elvira entered the room.

"All the palace is in excitement," she cried. "They say the Prince of Wales has arrived."

"It is perfectly true," replied the countess. "He arrived last night, but no announcement of the event was made till this morning."

"A singular circumstance occurred last night, which I cannot help connecting with the prince's arrival," said Doña Elvira. "There was a page in the palace who was unknown to all the other meninos, and no one can tell how he obtained admittance. We passed him as we left the great salon after the concert. Now I recollect, your highness spoke to him."

"Did I?" said the Infanta, quite unable to

ıde her confusion from the keen eye of the con-
ssor.

"Did your highness remark that he was a
ranger?" asked Padre Ambrosio.

"I took but little notice of him," she replied.
The Conde de Gondomar was with him."

"It was the prince in disguise—I am sure of it,"
uttered Padre Ambrosio. "Would your high-
ess know that page again if you beheld him?"
e asked.

"I should," interposed Doña Elvira.

Just then the door was thrown open, and the
ing entered the room.

"You have heard the news, Maria?" he cried
mbracing his sister, as she flew towards him.

"I have, sire," she replied.

"I make no doubt you are impatient to behold
our lover," he said. "You shall soon be gratified
ith a sight of him. I will engage him to drive
n the Prado this evening. You shall drive there

too, with the queen and myself, and then you can obtain a view of him as we pass his coach."

"I thank your majesty for your gracious consideration," replied the Infanta.

"I, myself, am most anxious to behold him," pursued Philip, "and would gladly have visited him at the casa of the Earl of Bristol, where he is lodged, but he stands punctiliously upon etiquette. With the romantic character he has displayed in this expedition, I almost wonder he did not present himself at the palace this morning, and solicit an interview with you, Maria."

"Your majesty is pleased to jest," replied the Infanta, blushing. "The prince must be too well aware of the rigorous etiquette practised at our court to transgress it."

"Humph!" muttered Padre Ambrosio.

"I long to behold the prince," remarked the Countess de Olivarez. "If he at all resembles his favourite, the Marquis of Buckingham, he must be very handsome."

"Yes, he is very handsome," echoed the Infanta, abstractedly.

"You speak as if you had seen him," remarked the king.

"I have his portrait, as you know, sire," she rejoined.

"Well, we shall all be able to judge of his appearance anon," said Philip. "He is reported to be the most chivalrous and accomplished prince in Europe, and I dare say he will not belie the description given of him. During the drive you must tie a white riband round your arm, Maria, so that the prince may know you."

"That precaution is scarcely necessary, methinks sire," observed Padre Ambrosio, with a certain significance. "The prince cannot fail to recognise her highness."

"Possibly not," rejoined the king, smiling. "But it is best to make sure. And now adieu, sweet sister. Prepare yourself for a sight of your future consort. I shall give orders that all the nobles of the court repair to the Prado this evening. You will be there, countess. I now go to acquaint her majesty with the unlooked-for occurrence."

With this, he again affectionately embraced his sister, and bowing to the countess, quitted the room.

"Stay with me awhile," whispered the Infanta to the countess. "I have more to say to you, and do not desire to be left alone with Doña Elvira and Padre Ambrosio."

"I will stay as long as you please," replied the countess.

IV.

OF THE VISIT PAID BY OLIVAREZ TO CHARLES.

Accompanied by Buckingham and Gondomar, and escorted by a mounted guard, as before, Olivarez drove to the House of Seven Chimneys, for the purpose of paying his homage to the prince.

On his arrival, the minister was ushered into the prince's presence with much ceremony by Buckingham. Charles was seated in a large tapestried hall, which served as a reception-chamber, and was surrounded at the moment by the Earl of Bristol, Sir Walter Aston, the ordinary ambassador to Madrid, and a man of considerable ability, young Harry Jermyn, Bristol's chief secretary, and Sir Richard Graham, Cottington, and Endymion Porter.

The prince had now abandoned his travelling attire, and wore the splendid court suit of white satin which he had procured in Paris. His head was covered with a broad-leaved Spanish hat, adorned with a diamond brooch and a white drooping plume. All his attendants were richly attired.

As the Conde-Duque, conducted by Buckingham and followed by Gondomar, drew near, Charles arose, and made a step towards him, with the evident design of preventing him from kneeling; but the minister would not be stayed, but threw himself at the prince's feet and kissed his hand, with every manifestation of reverence. When Charles at last raised him, and prayed him to be covered, he refused, though, as a grandee, he was entitled to wear his hat in the presence of his own sovereign. Gondomar paid a similar mark of respect to the prince, and remained uncovered.

"I am come," said Olivarez, in accents of the most profound respect, and with the most deferential demeanour, "in his majesty's name, to welcome your highness to Madrid. The visit was totally unexpected, but it is not the less gratifying on that account, and his majesty conceives himself placed under such deep obligation by the step taken by your highness that he can refuse you nothing."

"I hope I shall not ask more than he will be readily disposed to grant, my lord," replied Charles. "And yet it is in his majesty's power to confer the greatest possible favour upon me."

"Again I say, there is nothing your highness can ask that will be refused," replied Olivarez, bowing. "I should very imperfectly express his majesty's sentiments if I did not say so."

"I trust I shall soon have an opportunity of

thanking his majesty in person for his goodness," said Charles.

"His majesty desires to postpone the gratification of receiving your highness at the palace until arrangements can be made for your public entry into Madrid in a manner befitting your dignity. He would fain have visited you this morning, but my lord of Buckingham being opposed to that plan, the king relinquished the idea."

"Buckingham was right," said Charles. "I could not allow his majesty to visit me first."

"In this dilemma," said Olivarez, "his majesty proposes, if it meets with your highness's approval, that you shall drive in the Prado this evening, when he can have the opportunity he so eagerly desires of beholding you. He will come thither attended by the queen, the Infantes his brothers, and the Infanta."

"I entirely approve of the arrangement," remarked Charles. "But I trust his majesty will not allow the day to pass without affording me an opportunity of conversing with him and embracing him."

"Such, I am sure, is his majesty's intent, prince," replied Olivarez. "He is all impatience to greet you. He means to demonstrate his satisfaction at your highness's arrival by a series of triumphs and entertainments such as have never been exhibited in this capital since his majesty came to the throne. In order that the nobility of the court may appear in greater splendour, an edict recently passed against excess in attire shall be suspended. A quarter in the palace, in all respects like that occupied by the king, shall be assigned to your highness and your suite. You shall be attended by as many officers as the king, and be served in the same manner as his majesty. None beneath the rank and quality of a noble shall wait upon you. My brother-in-law, the Conde de Monterey, governor of Italy, a member of the council of state, and a grandee, shall be your mayor-domo-mayor. The Conde de Gondomar and the Duke de Cea shall also serve you as mayor-domos. Members of the council of state shall daily attend upon you to ascertain your pleasure; and four grandees—namely, Don Juan Alfonso Euriguez, Admiral of Castile, the Conde de Puebla, the Marquis de Velada, and the Duke de Yjar—shall be ever ready to accompany you when you desire to go abroad A royal guard of archers shall likewise serve as your escort."

"His majesty is far too gracious to me," said Charles.

"In regard to your highness's entry into the palace," pursued Olivarez, "his majesty desires that the solemnity shall be performed with as much pomp and splendour as would be observed at the coronation of a king of Castile. In accordance with this plan, your highness will be brought from the convent of San Geronimo, whence our kings re wont to make their solemn entry into the city, nd conducted by all the principal officers of state, ll the chief nobles of the court, and all the public fficers, to the palace."

"I lack words to express my gratitude," said Charles.

"Furthermore," pursued Olivarez, "in order iat all classes of the community may participate ı the joy felt by his majesty at your arrival, he ill proclaim a general pardon to all offenders. ll prisoners shall be set free."

"El Cortejo will have reason to thank your ighness, if he is included in the pardon," remarked uckingham.

"The royal signature will be given in blank to is highness," said Olivarez, "so that he can exend his grace to whomsoever he may please."

"I will not abuse the privilege," said Charles. I pray your excellency to thank the king most eartily for his great goodness towards me."

"I have but imperfectly described his majesty's intentions towards your highness," said Olivarez, "but I trust I have said enough to convince you of his earnest desire to please you. And now, having discharged my mission, I will take my leave of your highness."

So saying, the Conde-Duque withdrew with much ceremony.

V.

OW CHARLES DROVE IN THE PRADO, AND HOW HE SAW THE INFANTA IN THE CHAPEL OF THE RECOLETOS AGUSTINOS.

THOUGH naturally curious to behold the city, Charles did not stir forth during the day, but ccupied himself in writing a long letter to his oyal father, in which he acquainted him with his afe arrival in Madrid, and described his secret nterview with the Infanta, as he felt sure the occurrence would amuse the king. This done, and lespatched with another letter from Buckingham y a courier to England, the prince again strolled forth alone into the garden to indulge his meditations without interruption.

Later on, he dined in company with Buckingham and Gondomar. The Earl of Bristol waited upon him during the repast. Dinner over, he entered Gondomar's coach, and, attended by the conde, Buckingham, and Graham, drove to the Prado. The Earl of Bristol followed in his own coach, in which were seated Sir Walter Aston, Cottington, and Endymion Porter.

As the carriage containing the prince traversed the Calle de Alcala, on its way to the Prado, it passed the palace of the Conde-Duque de Olivarez, and Gondomar called Charles's attention to the magnificent edifice. In the court-yard, close to the grand entrance, stood the minister's superb coach, and near it was drawn up a mounted escort.

When the prince entered the Prado the drive was full of equipages, and the walks among the trees were crowded with richly-dressed caballeros ınd señoras. Nothing could be gayer than the cene. The evening was lovely, and seemed to ıave tempted forth the whole of the population ıf Madrid to this charming promenade.

But, besides the beauty of the evening, there ras another motive which had brought out all his concourse to the Prado. Promulgated at the alace, the rumour had gone abroad, and was cir-ulated with extraordinary rapidity throughout the ity, that the Infanta's suitor, the Prince of Wales, ad arrived, and would be seen in the Prado that vening. In consequence of this report, the Madri-ıños of all ranks flocked thither, in the hope of ıtching a glimpse of the illustrious stranger.

Nor were they disappointed. It soon became nown that the prince was in the Conde de Gon-omar's coach, and, as the equipage passed slowly long, all eyes were directed towards it, and Charles as readily distinguished. But the crowd were ːspectful and unobtrusive, and it being understood that the prince desired to remain incognito, they did not even attempt to cheer him. The noble physiognomy of the prince, his grave looks and dark complexion, delighted all beholders, and it was universally said that he looked like a Castilian Buckingham likewise attracted great attention, but was not so much admired as the prince.

In the central part of the drive, occupying the space between the Calle de Alcala and the Calle de San Geronimo, there was a broad open space, surrounded by benches, and terminated at either end by a fountain This spot, being resorted to by the best company, was known as the "Salon del Prado," a designation which it still retains. In the throng of caballeros careering round the ring, mounted on fiery jennets or beautiful Barbary horses, displaying their graces of horsemanship to the dark-eyed señoras seated on the benches or pacing to and fro on the walks, Charles beheld the chief gallants of the city. All that Madrid could produce in the way of splendour of equipage, of fashion and beauty, was to be seen at that moment in the Salon del Prado. There were stately hidalgos, richly-dressed cavaliers, and lovely dames, the latter, it may be mentioned, being universally attired in black, and wearing no other covering to the head except the graceful and becoming mantilla.

But, though the bulk of the crowd was composed of the higher classes, the populace was not excluded from the "Salon," and mingling with the gayest groups might be seen priests, monks, manolos, gitanos, and gallegos. Mounted archers were stationed at various points, but, as we have said, the demeanour of the crowd was so orderly, that their presence was scarcely required.

Charles had driven as far as Nuestra Señora de Atocha, a convent founded by Charles V., and situated at the eastern extremity of the Prado, and had just returned to the "Salon," when a grand procession of carriages, preceded by a mounted escort, was observed to be descending the slope from the Calle de Alcala. A hundred voices instantly called out, "The king!—the king!" And, on hearing these shouts, Gondomar at once ordered his coachman to halt.

Shortly afterwards the escort, which was proceeding at a foot's pace, rode by, and was followed by the king's carriage, the large windows of which being open, gave Charles a full view of the illustrious party inside it.

It was evident that Philip was anxiously looking out for the prince, and the moment he caught sight of him he courteously raised his hat, while Charles returned the salutation with equal respect. Not a word, of course, passed between the royal personages, but Philip's speaking glances conveyed the welcome he designed to accord to the prince.

Not less eloquent were the looks of all the rest of the party in the carriage. The Infanta thought the prince could read her heart as he gazed at her, and blushed deeply. The young queen, Elizabeth of France, was enraptured, and as soon as the carriage passed by, she exclaimed, with a glance at the Infanta, "Oh! how handsome he is!"

"By Santiago! he has a noble countenance," cried Philip. "And, strange to say, he looks more like a Spaniard than an Englishman."

The meeting had been watched with great interest by those sufficiently near to observe it, and loud shouts were now raised for the king, but with the good taste which had hitherto marked their proceedings, the crowd still abstained from any direct allusion to the prince.

After the royal carriage came that of the Conde-Duque, and the countess was in ecstasies at the sight of the prince. Then followed a dozen superb carriages belonging to the highest nobility of the court. All these equipages were splendidly gilt and painted, and made a magnificent show.

The grand cortége took its way slowly towards the Recoletos Agustinos, a monastery situated at the western extremity of the Prado, where the royal party designed to alight and pay their devotions, and Gondomar ordered his coachman to follow in the same direction.

Long before the prince's arrival, the royal family had entered the monastery. Charles nevertheless alighted, and was conducted to the chapel, where vespers were being solemnised. To this chapel only the royal family, and the nobles in immediate attendance upon the king, were admitted, but a word from Gondomar obtained instant entrance to Charles and his companions.

The scene that offered itself to Charles's gaze was striking. Within the chapel were congregated the first nobility of Spain, disposed in various groups. Before the altar knelt the young king, with the queen on his right, and the Infanta on the other side.

When Maria arose from prayer and looked round, the first object she beheld was her lover A thrill of joy passed through her frame, for she construed his presence in the chapel as a step towards Romanism, and felt sure he would soon worship at the same altar as herself. With more zeal than before, she resumed her devotions, but when she looked round again, Charles was gone.

Before the royal party issued from the monastery night had come on. But innumerable torches were lighted, and being borne by the side of the carriages on their return through the Prado, added greatly to the effect of the procession.

VI.

OF THE MEETING BETWEEN CHARLES AND THE KING IN THE PRADO.

On the prince's return to the House of Seven Chimneys, he found Olivarez awaiting his arrival.

"The glimpse which his majesty has obtained of your highness," said the minister, "so far from satisfying him, has awakened in his breast such an eager desire for an interview, that he cannot wait till to-morrow, and he hopes, therefore, that you will agree to meet him at midnight in the Prado."

"I am equally impatient to meet his majesty,"

returned Charles. "In what part of the Prado shall I find him?"

"Near the fountain at the east end," said Olivarez. "I shall be in attendance. I have a further request to prefer to your highness. It is, that you will graciously allow me to take the Marquis of Buckingham with me, so that on this occasion he may attend upon his majesty."

"Take him by all means," said Charles. "In return, the Conde de Gondomar shall attend upon me. To-night, my lord," he added to Buckingham, "you will consider yourself a Spaniard, and serve the king as faithfully as if you were his subject."

Thereupon, Olivarez and Buckingham quitted the room together.

A little before midnight, attended by Gondomar and the Earl of Bristol, Charles drove to the place of rendezvous appointed by the king. At that hour the Prado was almost deserted. An occasional coach, however, might be seen moving along slowly, while here and there a couple might be observed engaged in amorous converse.

The night was clear and starlight, and as Charles approached the fountain he perceived a coach drawn up near it. At a short distance from the carriage, pacing to and fro beneath the trees, could be seen a tall caballero, with his face muffled in his cloak, and a long rapier by his side. As soon as Gondomar caught sight of this personage, he said to Charles, "It is the king."

As the prince's coach stopped, the caballero became motionless, and waited till the prince drew near him. He then threw aside his cloak, and springing towards Charles, embraced him.

"My brother! I am delighted to meet you!" cried Philip.

"Sire, I am equally delighted to meet you," cried Charles.

For more than half an hour the two royal personages walked together among the trees, each with his arm round the other's neck, and both seemingly delighted at the meeting. Philip questioned Charles minutely as to his journey, and appeared greatly interested by all he heard. They also spoke of the Infanta, and Charles had every reason to believe that the king was quite as eager as himself for the speedy completion of the match.

So charmed were they with each other, that they were loth to separate. But when of necessity the interview came to an end, Philip begged permission to conduct the prince home. Charles with difficulty yielded, and it required some persuasion, and even a little gentle force on Philip's part, to induce the prince to get first into the carriage. "In doing this," he said, "I feel I am disobeying the king my father."

During the drive home Charles sat on the king's right, and although Olivarez and Buckingham were now present, their discourse was as friendly and as free from restraint as it had previously been. The king was very earnest with Olivarez to expedite as much as possible the preparations for the prince's public entry into the city and reception at the palace, and the Conde-Duque promised compliance.

By this time the carriage having arrived at the House of Seven Chimneys, the royal pair separated with every expression of regard.

VII

OF THE PRESENTS SENT TO CHARLES BY THE KING.

Thus far everything had gone well. Any misgivings that Charles entertained were banished from his breast, and gave place to joyful confidence. Unless some wholly unforeseen difficulty arose, it seemed impossible there could now be any serious impediment to the speedy completion of the treaty. Buckingham was quite as sanguine as the prince, and even Bristol, though he had so much experience of Spanish dissimulation, began to think that Olivarez meant to act fairly. Full of joyful anticipations of the future, Charles retired to rest.

Next morning, when Graham entered his chamber, and at the prince's request threw open the casement, the white dove, which had been perched on the window-sill since dawn, flew into the room, and alighted near the couch—so near, that Charles could have touched the beautiful bird if he had extended his hand. There it remained so long as the prince continued in the room.

On descending to the lower room Charles was informed that two large chests had just arrived from the palace, containing sumptuous apparel, and fine linen for himself and his attendants. Other presents were also sent by the king in the course of the day.

Among the few nobles who were presented that day to Charles by the Earl of Bristol was the Conde de Monterey, who, after kneeling and kissing the prince's hand, said,

"I have to inform your highness that it has just

een decided by the king and the council of state
hat your public entrance into the city shall take
lace at the earliest moment possible, his majesty
eing naturally anxious to have you as his guest
n the palace. The ceremonial has, therefore, been
xed for the day after to-morrow, and will be con-
ucted with the utmost splendour. On these oc-
asions it is customary for the kings and princes of
pain to make their entrance into the city on
orseback. Trusting, therefore, that your highness
vill deign to conform to the arrangement, his
najesty has sent by me two white Arabs of the
urest race, one of which he prays you to select for
our own use on the occasion—the other he him-
elf will ride."

"I will try them both, my lord," replied Charles,
ourteously, "and that which I deem the least ex-
ellent I will retain, leaving the other to the king.
pray you to convey my heartfelt thanks to his
najesty for the truly royal gifts he has lavished

upon me. I accept them as an evidence of his good will."

"I will deliver your highness's message," said Monterey, bowing profoundly. "Before I depart, let me entreat your highness to command my services in whatsoever way you may think proper. And, in making this offer, let me add that I speak not for myself, but for the whole court. All are equally devoted to your highness—all eager to serve you."

With another profound salutation, he then withdrew.

Charles's next visitor was the Duke de Cea, who had just arrived, and flew to pay his respects to the prince.

Charles received the young duke with great cordiality, and diverted him by relating what had happened to the two barbs. De Cea remarked that he had heard of El Cortejo as he crossed the Somosierra, but had not been molested by the robber-

;hief. After some further discourse, Charles withlrew with Bristol, leaving De Cea and Graham ılone together.

"I have news that will delight you, my dear 'riend," said the young duke. "I left Doña Casilda and her father at Fuencarrel. They will ;ome on to Madrid this evening, and to-morrow /ou can present yourself at the casa of the conde. But I cannot conceal from you that he *has* promised his daughter to Don Christobal. Do not, ıowever, be discouraged Doña Casilda prefers /ou to your rival. She owned as much to her ister, Doña Flor."

"You transport me with delight by what you ell me," cried Graham. "But where is Doña Flor?"

"She is with her father and sister, and will ırrive with them this evening. Don Pompeo oined them at Fuencarrel, and it was to avoid neeting him that I came on to Madrid. It seems that his suspicions have been aroused in regard to me, and I shall have to be doubly on my guard in future, for were he to make any discovery, his vengeance would know no bounds."

"For Doña Flor's sake, I think you ought to give up the affair," observed Graham.

"Impossible! I love her too well," said the young duke. "No, I must go on, be the risk what it may. But enough of this. I am curious to hear all that has happened to the prince since his arrival in Madrid."

Graham then entered into details, and described the prince's secret interview with the Infanta, with which De Cea was vastly amused.

"The stratagem does great credit to Gondomar," he said, with a laugh, "and was admirably carried out. I hope this will not be the only secret interview the prince will have with his mistress. When he takes up his abode in the palace other opportunities will occur. And as it appears that I am fortunate enough to be appointed one of his highness's lords in waiting, I shall be able to serve him in this respect."

Their conversation was here interrupted by the return of Charles and Bristol, and shortly afterwards Buckingham entered with Olivarez. The Conde-Duque came charged with the most cordial greetings of his royal master, who declared that he could not pass the day without beholding the prince, and therefore entreated his highness to pay him a private visit that evening in the palace.

To this Charles assented, all the more readily because he hoped to see the Infanta. But in that expectation he was disappointed.

Conveyed to the palace by Olivarez, he was met at the foot of a private staircase by his majesty, who was impatiently awaiting his arrival, and who led him to the garden, where they had an hour's conversation together.

At the close of the interview, the king attended Charles to his carriage, and when the prince had entered it his majesty leaped in, and insisted on accompanying him home.

VIII.

HOW THE PRINCE WENT TO THE CONVENT OF SAN GERONIMO.

At length the day arrived which had been appointed for the prince's public entrance into the city.

A little before noon, Charles and his attendants were assembled in the reception-chamber. The prince was attired in white satin, embroidered with gold. From his neck, sustained by a broad blue riband, hung the George, and beneath his knee he wore the enamelled Garter. All his attendants were attired in the sumptuous apparel sent by the King of Spain, and Buckingham's magnificent person was displayed to the greatest advantage in a doublet of orange-coloured satin, embroidered with leaves of silver, with a mantle to match. His cap was of black silk, enriched with pearls, and adorned with orange-coloured plumes.

Shortly afterwards four grandees were ushered in, all of whom were splendidly attired in cloths of gold and silver for the ceremonial. These were the Marquis de Montes Claros, Don Fernando Giron, the Conde de Gondomar, and the Duke de Cea. After making profound reverences to the prince, they informed him that, in pursuance of the king's orders, they were come to conduct his highness to the convent of San Geronimo.

Thanking them for their courtesy, Charles said he was ready to attend them. Whereupon, with as much ceremony as they could have shown to their own sovereign, they conducted him to a royal carriage which awaited him at the door of the mansion. Beside this superb equipage, which had half a dozen magnificently-caparisoned horses attached to it, there were two other coaches, and a detachment of mounted archers, in their full equipments, were drawn up, to act as an escort to the cortége.

Charles having entered the coach, Buckingham took a seat on his left, while Gondomar and De Cea sat opposite to them, with their backs to the horses. The next carriage was occupied by the Earl of Bristol, Sir Walter Aston, and the two grandees, and the third by the rest of Charles's attendants.

The cavalcade then got into motion, and made its way to the Calle de Alcala, which was crowded with people in their holiday attire. On beholding the carriage containing Charles, the throng called out lustily, "Viva el Principe de Galles!" Charles bowed repeatedly in acknowledgment of these demonstrations.

The royal convent of San Geronimo, whither

the prince was now proceeding, was a large monastic establishment, picturesquely situated on the rising ground on the north side of the Prado, in the midst of the wood. From this convent it was customary for the kings of Castile to make a public entry into the city on the occasion of their coronation, and no greater honour could have been shown to Charles by the Spanish nation than to treat him as one of their own kings.

At the gate of the convent stood the lord prior, ready to receive the prince as he alighted, and all the brethren who were assembled in the hall bowed reverently as Charles passed through it. Having ceremoniously conducted his illustrious guest to the royal apartments, the lord prior left him, and proceeded with the brethren to the chapel, where mass was performed.

Breakfast was then served for Charles and his attendants, and the prince was waited upon by the grandees precisely as Philip himself would have been served.

When the repast was concluded, Charles repaired to the audience-chamber, where a chair of state had been prepared for him, on which he took his seat—the Spanish grandees standing on his right hand, and Buckingham and Bristol on the left. The prince had now to give audience to various important personages, in the same manner as the king. The first to be introduced was the Inquisidor General—a tall, dark man, who seemed well fitted by his looks for the office he held. Nevertheless, he bent reverently before the heretical prince, and respectfully kissed his highness's hands.

As the Inquisidor General moved on and took his place near the grandees, he was succeeded by the members of the Council-Royal of Castile, all of whom knelt before the prince, those nearest him kissing his hand. Then came the Council-Royal of Aragon; then the Council of Portugal; and after them the Council of Italy, the Council of Military Orders, the Council of the Indies, the

Council of the Treasury, and the Council of the Exchequer. Lastly, came Don Juan de Castilla, the Corregidor of Madrid, and Don Lorenzo Olivarez, Don Pedro de Torres, and Don Christobal de Medina, the three principal Regidores. All these important officers knelt before the prince, and after kissing his hand, drew up on either side of the chair of state.

Just as the ceremonial was completed, loud fanfares of trumpets were heard without, and the usher announced that the king and his two royal brothers had arrived at the convent.

On this intelligence Charles immediately arose, and followed by the grandees, together with Buckingham and Bristol, proceeded to the gate of the convent, where he found Philip, who had just alighted with the two Infantes. On seeing Charles, the king flew towards him, and affectionately embraced him.

The two young princes next embraced Charles,

after which the royal party returned to the audience-chamber. Here the king and his brothers stood on one side, while all the grandees, nobles, and gentlemen who had attended his majesty, passed before Charles, and kissed his hand.

This done, trumpets were sounded, and a herald came forward, proclaiming that, in honour of the visit of the Prince of Wales, a general pardon would be granted by his majesty to all offenders. With a profound obeisance to the prince, the herald then went forth to make the proclamation in different parts of the city.

On his departure, the heads of each of the councils advanced towards the prince, and, when they had stationed themselves before him, Philip, who was standing beside Charles, spoke thus:

"Desiring to show all honour to the illustrious Prince of Wales, who is now our guest, we enjoin you, our faithful councillors, and all magistrates and public officers, to do no favour and bestow no office, without his highness's direction, during his abode with us."

"Your majesty's commands shall be obeyed," replied the chief of the Council of Castile, speaking for the rest.

The whole assemblage then shouted, as with one voice, "Viva el Principe de Galles!"

Bowing graciously around, in token of his satisfaction, Philip next took the hand of Charles, and led him to the room in which he had breakfasted. They were followed by the two young princes. While the royal party tarried in this inner room, cates and conserves, with sweet wines of Malaga and Alicante, were served to them by the monks.

IX.

OF THE PNINCE'S PUBLIC ENTRY INTO MADRID.

Meantime, the procession had set forth from the convent. At its head rode a band of trumpets and clarions, drums, kettle-drums, cymbals, and fifes, making the air resound with martial strains. The musicians wore cassocks of carnation satin guarded with silver lace, and having black borders cut upon silver tinsel. Their caps were of black velvet adorned with black and carnation plumes. They were all well mounted, and had the royal arms embroidered on the housings of their horses, banners, and pennons.

Next came four trumpeters belonging to the city of Madrid, clad in cassocks of orange-coloured taffata laid with silver lace, and wearing black hats adorned with plumes of the same hue as their cassocks. They were followed by a great host of lacqueys habited in similar liveries, each armed with sword and dagger, and carrying a white buckler.

Next came the three Regidores riding together, and the Corregidor riding by himself.

After them came four trumpeters belonging to Don Juan Alfonso Eurigucz, Admiral of Castile, in long coats of black satin guarded with gold lace, with the admiral's arms on their breasts, and wearing black hats with yellow and white plumes.

The admiral, who was mounted on a richly-trapped charger, and bore a silver staff, was preceded by fifty lacqueys, wearing doublets of black satin, cloaks fringed with gold, white shoes, and black hats with orange and white plumes.

Then came four trumpeters belonging to Don 'edro de Toledo-Osorio, Marquis of Villa Franca, earing gaberdines of yellow satin laid with gold ice, with the arms of the house of Toledo woven n their breasts and shoulders. Their hats were f black taffeta, with bands of gold and white lumes.

Don Pedro was preceded by thirty mounted icqueys in doublets laid with gold lace, with leeves of tinsel, and hats embroidered with little rindmills of gold, and adorned with white plumes nd tucks of silver.

Next came four trumpeters belonging to the Conde de Monterey, with cassocks of white satin, aced and flowered with gold, hats of white satin with black plumes, and having the conde's arms mbroidered on their bandrols.

De Monterey was preceded by a hundred acqueys, mounted on horses trapped with white ind gold, being the colours of the Prince of

Wales, and habited in white satin, adorned with leaves of gold, and wearing black hats with black and white plumes.

Next came the trumpeters of the Duke de Cea, in cassocks of blue satin laid with silver, black hats with blue plumes, and having the duke's arms on their trumpets. Before the duke rode fifty lacqueys, mounted on noble chargers, with trappings of velvet adorned with pearls, and having pouncings of gold, silver, and pomegranates. These lacqueys bore white targets with white bandels, and were attired in blue satin covered with silver lace. Their hats were of black satin, with bands of silver and blue plumes.

Next came the trumpeters of Don Juan Hurtado de Mendoza, Duke de Infantado, one of the proudest of the Castilian nobles. These men wore white frizado mantles, with gaberdines of black damask edged with silver lace, with the arms of Mendoza on their shoulders and breasts,

well as on the bandrols of their clarions. Before
ie old duke rode fifty lacqueys in doublets and
ose of black satin, guarded with broad silver lace,
id black velvet hats with bands and wreaths of
lver, and black and white plumes. Behind him
ode fifty grooms in crimson taffeta. The horses
ere trapped in black and white.

After these followed the trumpeters and lacqueys
' Don Diego Lopez de Zuniga, General of the
oast of Granada. Next those of Don Fernando
iron. Then those of the Marquis of Castel Ro-
rigo; those of the Castellan of the Cordovas; of
ie Marquis del Carpio; of the Conde de Saldana,
on Christobal de Gavina, the Conde de Gondo-
iar, and a multitude of others.

The grandees vied with each other in splendour
f habiliments and number of attendants.

After the nobles and their attendants had ridden
n, there came a dozen trumpeters in carnation
itin, with the royal arms woven in gold on their

bandiols. They were followed by the king's equerry, his majesty's riders, the royal pages and officers.

Then followed a hundred gentlemen of the royal household, each mounted on a goodly charger, trapped in black and white, with silver musrols, and coverings of crimson velvet, fringed with gold thread. On these cloths were embroidered the king's name, Felipe IV., with the royal blazon.

Holding the bridle of each horse was a footman in a doublet of carnation satin, laid with silver and black lace, with mantles of cloth of silver. Their hats were black, with silver bands and carnation and black plumes. Then followed the mayor-domos, and after them came the king and the Prince of Wales riding side by side, Charles being placed on his majesty's right hand. Both presented a most majestic appearance—both were perfect horsemen, so that it was impossible to say to whom the palm of superior grace ought to be assigned. Philip was attired in black taffeta richly guarded. His girdle glittered with diamonds, and his black velvet hat, which was surmounted by tall white plumes, was ornamented with priceless jewels. Round his neck was a massive chain of gold, ornamented with green and black emeralds, and representing four crowns linked together. He also wore the orders of the Toison d'Or and Calatrava, and on his mantle was embroidered the red cross of Santiago. The trappings and furniture of the two noble steeds were exactly alike. The manes and tails of the animals were plaited with gold, the bridles and saddles were of red morocco leather embroidered with magnificent pearls, covered with the finest lambskins, and the housings were of crimson velvet, garnished and guarded with gold lace.

Behind the two royal personages, mounted on chargers trapped in crimson velvet, embroidered with gold, and adorned with their arms, rode Olivarez and Buckingham, side by side like Philip and Charles—and apparently, from their looks and gestures, the best friends in the world. On this occasion the two favourites acted as masters of the horse to their respective rulers, and each was accompanied by a richly-caparisoned charger, led by a couple of grooms, as a symbol of his office.

Buckingham's habiliments have been already described. Those of Olivarez were of black satin embroidered with gold, and cut upon silver tinsel, and the haughty minister wore a black hat glittering with diamonds, and adorned with black plumes striped with gold.

A crowd of richly-attired pages followed. Then came the Earl of Bristol and Sir Walter Aston, followed by Charles's three attendants, Graham, Cottington, and Endymion Porter, all of whom made a gallant show. The rear of the long and magnificent cortége was brought up by a detachment of the Almayn guard, under the command of the Conde de Barrajas.

The setting forth of Philip and Charles from the Convent of San Geronimo was announced by a peal of ordnance, and thereupon all the bells of the city began to ring joyously. Thousands of persons were collected in the Prado to witness the procession, and their continuous shouts rent the air. When Philip and Charles came in sight, these acclamations were redoubled.

After traversing the Salon del Prado, the cortége proceeded to the Calle de Alcala, and as the king and the prince approached the street, four-and-twenty regidores of the city, gorgeously arrayed in cloth of tissue, met them, bearing a superb canopy, which they held over the king and his guest during their progress through the city. We may mention that this superb canopy was afterwards presented by the regidores to Buckingham.

From the court-yard of the palace of the Conde-Duque three hundred gentlemen in the minister's livery, and bearing his arms, and all well mounted, came forth to join the procession. They were under the command of Don Luis de Haro, son of the Marquis del Carpio, and nephew of the Conde-Duque.

As may be supposed, the Calle de Alcala was densely crowded, but a road was preserved for the cavalcade by mounted archers and arquebusiers. In the widest part of the street, beyond the palace of the Conde-Duque, large scaffolds were erected, covered with rich cloths and tapestry, and these were now occupied by the various councils and important functionaries who had just been to pay homage to the prince.

All the habitations were decorated with costly stuffs, cloths of gold and silver, carpets and hangings, and, in some cases, pictures were hung out. The balconies and windows were filled with fair spectators, who waved their kerchiefs as the king and prince passed by. Not even at Philip's coronation had so much enthusiasm been displayed. Poems were improvised in the prince's honour, and the following refrain to a song, composed for the occasion by the famous Lope de Vega, was everywhere chanted:

> Carlos Estuardo soy,
> Que, siendo amor mi guia,
> Al cielo de España voy
> Por ver my estrella Maria.

Charles Stuart was indeed the hero of the hour. The story of his romantic expedition had been everywhere recounted, and had roused the strongest sympathies of a generous and impulsive people. The prince's distinguished appearance and majestic deportment more than realised the notions that had been formed of him, and all tongues were loud in his praise. Moreover, it had been artfully insinuated by the priesthood, at the instigation of Olivarez, that not only had Charles come to claim the Infanta, but that he intended to recant his heresies and embrace the faith of Rome, and this fiction being firmly believed by the populace, there was no drawback to the general rejoicing.

At the Puerta del Sol a stage was erected, on

which was performed a ballet, introducing the best national dances. The fountain in the midst of the plaza ran with wine, and all the houses in the Calle Mayor were as richly adorned as those in the Calle de Alcala.

As he entered the grand plaza in front of the Palacio Real, a magnificent spectacle was offered to the prince. The whole of the cavalcade was here drawn up, and was surrounded by the royal guard in their full accoutrements. The clangour of the trumpet, the clash of the cymbal, the thunder of the kettle-drum, and the shrill notes of the fife, were heard from the band which was stationed near the principal gate of the palace. Towards this gate, which we have already mentioned retained its original Moorish character, Philip and Charles now proceeded amid the deafening acclamations of the spectators.

At the gate they were met by Don Luis de Paredes, alcayde of the palace, with a number of gentlemen of the household, and were ceremoniously conducted to the grand portal, where the king and his royal guest alighted. Fain would Charles have taken the hindmost place, but this Philip would not permit, and the point of etiquette was at last adjusted, as it had been before, by their walking side by side, each with an arm on the other's shoulder. In this fraternal fashion, which excited the admiration of all who beheld them, and preceded by the Conde de Puebla and the Conde de Benavente, mayor-domos, they repaired to her majesty's quarter.

They found the queen in a large and splendidly furnished apartment, at the upper end of which was a canopy of gold tissue adorned with the arms of Castile and Aragon. On either side of the canopy were ranged the queen's meninos and meninas, habited in rose-coloured satin, and beneath it were placed gilt chairs, covered with crimson velvet, on which the queen and the Infanta were seated, but on the entrance of Charles with the king, the two royal ladies at once arose and advanced to meet him.

Her majesty was splendidly arrayed in a robe of cloth of silver, and literally blazed with diamonds. The Infanta was far more simply attired in white satin, and her sole ornaments were pearls. She blushed deeply as she returned Charles's profound salutation, and when addressed by him she trembled and manifested considerable agitation. The prince augured well from this display of feeling. The royal party next proceeded to the canopy, where Charles was placed between the queen and the Infanta, and where they all remained for some time in conversation. But in spite of his efforts, Charles failed to draw the Infanta into discourse. She listened with evident interest to what he said, and sometimes smiled, but silence seemed imposed upon her by the frigid rules of Spanish etiquette. On the other hand, the queen was extremely lively.

Half an hour was spent in this way, and at the expiration of that time his majesty proposed to conduct the prince to his quarter of the palace. As Charles withdrew, the queen and the Infanta accompanied him to the door.

A magnificent suite of apartments, equal in extent to those occupied by his majesty, had been assigned to the prince. They were situated in that part of the palace which enjoyed the finest view, and overlooked the gardens and the valley of the Manzanares. At the back was a patio surrounded by marble arcades, and filled with orange-trees. When the king and the prince entered the noble gallery belonging to the apartments in question, they were met by the Conde de Monterey, who had been appointed the prince's mayor-domo-mayor, and the Conde de Gondomar and the Duke de Cea, his highness's mayor-domos, and were ceremoniously ushered into a grand reception-chamber, where they found the Conde-Duque de Olivarez, the Duque de Infantado, the Admiral of Castile, the Marquis del

Castel Rodrigo, and all the first grandees of Spain. With them were the Marquis of Buckingham, the Earl of Bristol, Sir Walter Aston, Graham, and the rest of Charles's attendants.

The grandees raised their hats to Charles, but immediately replaced them.

While the royal pair were still standing together, the Conde de Monterey delivered two gold keys to his majesty, who took them, and, presenting them to Charles, said:

"These keys will open all the doors of the palace to you. Your highness will bestow them as you deem meet."

Returning suitable thanks, Charles immediately gave one key to Buckingham, and the other to Bristol.

Shortly afterwards, the large doors at the upper end of the chamber were thrown open, and an usher announced that the banquet was served.

Amid flourishes of trumpets, and marshalled by the Conde de Monterey and the two other mayor-domos, Philip and Charles, walking side by side, passed into the banqueting-chamber, where a grand repast awaited them.

At the upper end of the long table, on which was a gorgeous display of gold plate, was a dais, with a canopy above it emblazoned with the arms of England. Here seats were placed for Philip and Charles, who were waited upon by Gondomar and De Cea.

At the close of the banquet, the king and prince, with all the court, drove forth to witness the rejoicings that were taking place in the city. When night came on, all the houses were illuminated, and immense bonfires were lighted in the public places. At midnight, a grand display of fireworks took place in the Salon del Prado.

With shouts of welcome ringing in his ears, Charles returned to his apartments in the Palacio Real.

End of the Third Book.

BOOK IV.

FIESTAS REALES

I.

HOW CHARLES PASSED HIS TIME AT THE PALACE.

For more than a fortnight Charles had now occupied the magnificent suite of apartments assigned him by the king in the royal palace. He was treated with as much state and ceremony as Philip himself, served by grandees, consulted by the heads of the different councils and other officials, attended by a princely retinue of servants, and escorted by a guard of mounted archers whenever he stirred abroad. During all this time the royal festivities had continued, and splendid entertainments were given, at which the whole court assisted. Rejoicings were also held throughout the city, and bonfires blazed nightly in all the public places.

Nothing was talked about but the approaching royal marriage, and it was universally believed that the ceremonial was only delayed until the prince had publicly abjured his heresies, and conformed to the faith of Rome. The latter opinion was somewhat shaken by the arrival of two English chaplains, Doctors Man and Wren. These Protestant divines were regarded with so much dislike at the palace, that they were compelled to take up their abode with the Earl of Bristol at the House of Seven Chimneys.

By this time so many English nobles and persons of distinction had arrived in Madrid, that Charles was able to keep up a court of his own at the palace, and his ante-chamber was daily crowded. Among the first to join the prince were the Earl of Carlisle, with the Lords Mountjoy and Kensington, each of whom brought with him a retinue of servants and a supply of horses. The next to arrive were Lord Andover and Sir Robert Carr, gentlemen of the bed-chamber to the prince. Next came Lord Vaughan, the prince's comptroller, and with him Archie, the court fool, who had claimed fulfilment of James's promise to allow him to visit Madrid. Then came Lords Hay, Rochford, and Montague, with Sir George Goring, Sir Thomas Jermyn, Sir John Wentworth, and many others, bringing with them rich habiliments, tilting furniture, horses, jewels, and other ornaments for the prince and Buckingham, who were thus enabled to make a display befitting their dignity.

Buckingham also was gratified in an especial manner. A patent, by which he was created Earl of Coventry and Duke of Buckingham, was sent him by his royal master. Sir Francis Steward, the bearer of the patent, also brought with him the insignia of the Garter for the newly-made duke, together with the gorgeous robes of the Order, to be worn by the prince and Buckingham on Saint George's Day.

"I send you also," wrote James to his two bairns, "the robes of the Order, which you must not forget to wear on Saint George's Day, and dine together in them, if they come in time, which I pray God they may, for it will be a goodly sight for the Spaniards to see my two boys dine in them."

The accession of rank which he had thus acquired was especially gratifying to Buckingham, as it placed him on a level with Olivarez. But his arrogance was greatly increased, and became almost insufferable. Though Olivarez unquestionably exercised as much influence over Philip as Buckingham did over Charles, the haughty minister treated his royal master with every outward show of respect. Not so Buckingham, who even ventured to eat himself in the prince's presence—an unpardon-.ble breach of etiquette in the opinion of the ;randees, who could not understand how the prince olerated such familiarity. Nothing but considera-ion for Charles prevented many of them, provoked .lmost beyond endurance by the favourite's inso-ence, from coming to an open rupture with him. 3uckingham, however, seemed utterly indifferent o their opinion, regarding the Spaniards with ill-lisguised scorn, and treating them with unbecoming evity. In the midst of a grave discussion he vould break off suddenly with the snatch of a ong, as if to manifest the little impression pro-luced upon him by the conference, or, snapping his ingers like castanets, would amuse himself by prac-.ising a bolero or a seguidilla. After a time, the)nly influential person in the Spanish cabinet who :emained constant to him was the Conde de Gon-lomar.

Digby's grave and courteous manners were

favourably contrasted with those of Buckingham, and general regret was expressed that the prince did not prefer him to the capricious, frivolous, and overbearing favourite. In the hope of lowering Bristol in the esteem of the Spanish cabinet and court, Buckingham lost no opportunity of slighting him; but he did not succeed in his design, and had the mortification of discovering that the discreet ambassador was preferred to himself by the king and his minister.

This dissension between Buckingham and his colleague was singularly unfortunate for Charles, as it rendered unanimity in his councils impossible; any proposition made by Bristol, however judicious, being opposed by Buckingham. Hence constant difficulties were created.

But while Buckingham was raising up against himself a host of enemies, and the English nobles, aping his manner, were rendering themselves obnoxious to the Spaniards by their insolence, Charles lost none of his popularity. His gracious manner and dignified deportment delighted all who approached him; and so friendly was the intercourse between him and the king, that Philip began to feel a real affection for his expected brother-in-law. The two exalted personages rode forth frequently together, and amused themselves with hawking on the plains in the valley of the Manzanares, or in chasing the wild-boar, the wolf, and the fox, in the woods of a royal domain called El Pardo, about three or four leagues from Madrid.

But though Charles had every reason to be satisfied with the attention shown him by the king, he was wofully disappointed in the main object of his visit. His suit with the Infanta made little or no progress. He saw her daily, it is true, either at some grand entertainment in the palace, or in the royal carriage when she drove in the Prado; but he found it impossible to obtain any private discourse with her. Her manner towards him was so constrained and formal that he was almost driven to despair. De Cea had undertaken to obtain him a private interview with her, but since the prince's arrival at the palace she had been so closely watched, that hitherto the young duke had failed in the attempt.

So annoyed was Charles by the treatment he experienced, that one day he remonstrated on the subject with the king.

"I fear my visit will be in vain, sire," he said. "I cannot flatter myself that I make the slightest progress in your sister's good graces. I know not how to express myself otherwise than by saying that she surrounds herself with an icy atmosphere that chills me as I approach. As her accepted suitor, methinks I ought to be allowed somewhat greater freedom."

"I admit the justice of your complaint, prince," said Philip, "but it is not in my power to relax in the slightest degree the forms prescribed by tiquette in regard to my sister. But rest assured, hough her manner is necessarily cold and formal, n reality she is strongly attached to you."

"I should feel perfectly easy if I could have ıch an assurance from her own lips, sire," 1e-ıarked Charles.

"It is impossible she can so satisfy you until after ıe espousals, when her position will be altered," ıid Philip. "Meantime, I am aware of her senti-ıents, and can speak for her"

Charles made no reply, but said to himself, "I 'ill see her at all hazaıds."

II.

MADRID FROM THE MONTAÑA DEL PRINCIPE PIO.

On the morning after the conversation just recorded took place between the king and the prince, at an early hour three persons of noble mien ascended the path leading to the summit of the Montaña del Principe Pio, a hill situated at the north-west side of Madrid.

Apparently their object was to obtain a view of the city, which the eminence in question afforded, for as soon as they had selected an advantageous position, they stood still and gazed around, careılly noting the various objects that came under ıeir observation.

On the brow of the hill, immediately in their ːar, and completely commanding the city with its ːdnance, was a strong square fort surrounded by ımparts. From a standard planted on the highest oint of this redoubt the royal banner floated in the ıorning breeze, while armed men paced to and fro n the walls.

We have already mentioned that it was not until 'hilip II. fixed his residence in Madrid that it beıme the capital of Spain, and it was chiefly during is reign and that of his son, Philip III., that the ty had been extended and embellished. Hence, ' at the period of our history Madrid could boast f little antiquity, it had other merits in the eyes f the persons who now regarded it. Well built, ıid out with a certain regularity, it had several road and handsome streets, many noble plazas dorned with fountains and statues, a large park, and royal gardens, to which the public had access. The architecture of its habitations, if not picturesque, had an imposing character, and many of the palaces of the nobility were of vast size and very stately appearance.

From the Montaña del Principe Pio, which was only separated by a valley from the palace, an admirable view of that truly regal structure was obtained. Indeed, from no other spot could it be seen to so much advantage. From the same heights, also, the royal gardens were discernible, as well as the Casa del Campo, a delightful country residence belonging to the king on the farther side of the shallow Manzanares.

The attention, however, of the three persons was chiefly engrossed by the city. After counting the gates, commencing with the Puerta de Segovia, which was a little to the south of the palace, passing on to the Puerta de Toledo, and thence to the Puerta de Atocha, they followed the Prado till they came to the Puerta de Alcala, and completed their survey with the Puerta de Bilboa. All the more prominent features of the city were thus brought before them, and they were enabled to form an accurate notion of its general appearance and extent.

One of the party, who acted as cicerone to the others, next pointed out the principal streets—the Calle de Alcala and the Calle Mayor, which traversed the city from east to west, running from the Prado to the royal palace—the Calle de Atocha, the Calle de Geronimo, and the Calle de Toledo. Having traced the streets, they turned to the plazas, and readily distinguished those of San Joachim, La Cevado, and San Domingo, the Puerta del Sol, and the Plaza Mayor. The churches and convents next claimed attention, and the guide pointed out San Domingo el Real, founded in the thirteenth century; Nuestra Señora de la Concepcion, built at the close of the fifteenth century; the monastery of the Descalzes Reales, founded by Juana, daughter of Charles V.; La Encarnacion, built some years previously by Margaret of Austria, mother of Philip IV.; and several others—none of them, however, with much pretension to architectural beauty. From streets, plazas, churches, and public buildings, the guide came to private mansions, and while pointing out the residences of the chief nobility, indicated the abode of Don Pompeo de Tarsis in the Calle Ancha de San Bernardo, the Casa Saldana, and, lastly, the House of Seven Chimneys.

Their survey of the city completed, the party suffered their gaze to stray over its environs. In the bare and tawny plain in which Madrid is situated there is little on which the eye can rest with pleasure—no green pastures, no woods, nothing but a vast tract of stony country, dreary and desolate almost as a wilderness. There was scarcely any water in the channel of the Manzanares—the only

iver to be seen in the neighbourhood. An impres-
ive aspect, however, was given to the vast stony
plains by the ranges of lofty snow-clad mountains
by which they were bounded; and though these
mountainous chains—the Somosierra and the Gua-
larrama—were many leagues off, the atmosphere
was so clear that the rifts on their sides and their
agged peaks could be clearly distinguished. More-
over, amid this stony waste there were a few
green spots. A forest could here and there be seen,
with a hunting-seat attached to it. These forests
formed part of the royal domains, and abounded
with wild-boar and deer. El Pardo Zarsuela, to
which the king often resorted to recreate himself
with the chase, was pointed out by the cicerone,
who also showed his companions another beautiful
country-seat belonging to Philip, called La Florida.
Lastly, he directed their attention to the king's
favourite retreat, El Buen Retiro, situated at the

east side of the Prado, and renowned for its delightful gardens.

Upwards of an hour having been spent in this survey of the city and its environs, the person who had acted as cicerone on the occasion, and who was no other than the Conde de Gondomar, said to the chief of his companions:

"Is there anything further I can show your highness?"

"No, I am quite satisfied," replied Charles. "I have now got as perfect a notion of Madrid as if I had dwelt all my life in the city."

"What think you of the city, my lord duke?" inquired Gondomar, turning to the other.

"I like it better than I did at first," returned Buckingham. "But I hope I shall not offend you, count, if I confess that I am a little disappointed."

"Offend me! not in the least," replied Gondomar, smiling. "I can bear to hear Madrid abused without feeling my self-love hurt. Nay, I am so nuch of an Englishman, that I prefer London. Still, I think it a fine city."

"So it is," cried Charles, "a very fine city. Those lofty mountains, with their snowy peaks—ven the bare plains by which it is surrounded—dd greatly to its effect. If it has no monuments f antiquity—no picturesque structures replete with istorical associations—it has at least broad streets, pacious plazas, and noble habitations. Above all, t has a magnificent palace."

"To say nothing of a river without water," re-narked Buckingham. "I see the bed of the Ianzanares, but can discern no stream."

"The channel is dry now," said Gondomar. "But at times it contains a torrent. If your high-ess is satisfied, we will proceed to the Casa del Campo. It is about the hour when the Infanta vill go there."

"Is it not too early as yet?" remarked Charles.

"The princess rises betimes," returned Gondomar, "and the morning is so fine that it is certain to tempt her forth. I will engage you shall see her."

"Nay then, let us not tarry a moment longer," cried Charles.

III.

LA CASA DEL CAMPO.

THE party then hastily descended the hill, and proceeded along a road skirting the walls of the royal gardens, laid out on the ancient Campo del Moro. This road brought them to a handsome stone bridge across the Manzanares, or rather across the almost dry bed of that generally insignificant stream. Opposite them, on the farther bank of the river, was the Casa del Campo, a small palace belonging to the king, the chief attraction of which was its charming garden.

To this delightful retreat the Infanta frequently repaired in the early morning, when she was likely to be unobserved. Just as Charles and his attendants had crossed the bridge, two royal carriages were seen approaching, and the prince, whose beating heart informed him that his mistress was at hand, stepped out of the road to allow them to pass.

As he had anticipated, the first carriage contained the princess. She was attended by Doña Elvira and the old Duke del Infantado. As Charles caught her eye, she at once recognised him, and uttered a cry of delight and surprise, but her vivacity was quickly checked by the severe looks of Doña Elvira.

"It is the prince!" exclaimed Maria.

"The prince!" echoed the old duke, in surprise, and with a look of displeasure. "What is he doing abroad at this hour? You did not expect to behold him, princess?"

"Certainly not," she replied.

"He cannot be admitted to the casa while you are there, princess," said Doña Elvira. "I will not allow any meeting between you."

"The prince has no such design, I am quite sure," said the Infanta.

"I hope not," rejoined Doña Elvira, severely. "But I shall take measures to prevent it."

"Quite right, señora," remarked the old duke, approvingly.

By this time the carriage had reached the casa, and was driven into the court-yard, where the princess and the two persons with her alighted. The second coach contained four meninas, who likewise alighted and followed the princess into the palace. Doña Elvira's first order was that the outer gates should be immediately closed, and no one, of whatever rank, or under any pretext, admitted during the stay of the Lady Infanta.

"These precautions are quite unnecessary," said

the Infanta, scarcely able to conceal her vexation; "but I suppose you feel bound to take them."

"His majesty would blame me if anything occurred," replied Doña Elvira.

"You cannot be too particular, señora," said the duke.

The Infanta made no remark, but passing through the open windows of a saloon, entered the garden. Evidently anxious to be alone, she walked quickly on, and as Doña Elvira was now quite free from apprehension, she did not attempt to hasten after her, but followed at a leisurely pace with the old duke. The meninas, enchanted to be freed from restraint, scattered themselves in different directions, and began to gather flowers.

Meantime, the Infanta continued to hurry on until she reached a more retired part of the garden. She was pursuing a shady path, when a noise attracted her attention, and she perceived a man on the summit of the garden wall. It was the prince.

A cry escaped her at the sight, and she hardly knew whether to remain or fly. While she was in this state of indecision, Charles leaped lightly to the ground, and hastened towards her.

"Fortune indeed has favoured me, princess," he cried, flinging himself on his knee before her and taking her hand. "I have entered this retreat, scarcely hoping to find you, but chance has brought me to you at once."

"You have done wrong to come here at all, prince," she rejoined. "But you must not stay. I would not have you discovered for the world. Strict orders have been given by Doña Elvira that you are not to be admitted to the casa, and if she finds you here she will think the meeting has been preconcerted."

"Let her think what she pleases, Maria," cried Charles. "I will not go. I cannot tear myself from you. I am never able to obtain a moment's private converse with you — never allowed to breathe my passion to you. Why should I be treated with all this form and coldness? Am I not your suitor? Why, then, should I be debarred from approaching you?"

"Because such is the custom in this court, prince," she replied. "A princess of the royal blood of Spain is not allowed any interchange of affection with her suitor until after their espousals. It is against her honour, and would be accounted a reproach to her to see him alone. I must, therefore, beseech you to leave me instantly."

"Thus enjoined, I must needs obey you, Maria," cried Charles, rising.

"Stay, prince," she exclaimed, checking him. "I would not have you think me indifferent to you. Etiquette compels me to hide my feelings—to treat you as a stranger, with coldness and reserve. But I find it a hard part to play. Pity me, Charles—pity me—but do not blame me."

"Then you do love me, Maria?" he cried, rapturously.

"Can you doubt it, Charles, after what I have just said?" she replied, with a tenderness in her accents which they had never before betrayed. "But since nothing less will content you, I will own that I love you—love you dearly."

"My doubts are dispelled. My happiness is complete," cried the prince. "Oh! Maria, all I have undergone for your sake is more than requited."

"Oh, Charles!" she rejoined. "Henceforth you will understand me better. If I am compelled to act coldly towards you—to remain mute when you address me—you will know what is passing within. You will forgive me."

"You are an angel," he exclaimed.

And, carried away by his passion, he clasped her in his arms.

In an instant all the chains that etiquette had bound around the Infanta were broken. She did not attempt to disengage herself from her lover's embrace, but looked up tenderly in his face. Thus did they gaze at each other for a moment, and then their lips met.

"Maria, my beloved, I thus vow eternal fidelity to you," he cried.

"Charles, I am yours for ever. I swear it!" she rejoined, with equal fervour.

Thinking only of themselves, forgetting all the world beside, utterly unconscious of danger, they were still gazing fondly at each other, when the Infanta suddenly started.

"Fly, prince!" she cried. "Footsteps are approaching."

"A minute longer!" he implored.

"Not a second," she rejoined, "or we shall be discovered."

Scarcely were the words uttered than Doña Elvira and the Duke del Infantado issued from a side-path. If some dreadful spectacle had met her sight the dueña could not have looked more aghast.

"Holy Mother!" she exclaimed, with a scream. "Look, duke! look! There they are together. Oh! I shall expire."

"Compose yourself, señora. You will have need of all your faculties," cried the old duke.

IV.

THE DUKE DEL INFANTADO.

For a few moments no movement was made on either side. Doña Elvira did not advance, expecting the Infanta to come to her, but the princess did not stir, neither did Charles relinquish her hand. The Duke del Infantado, whom we have already described as one of the proudest of the Castilian nobles, then stepped forward, and, making a profound obeisance to the Infanta, said,

"Permit me, princess, to conduct you to your governess."

She made no reply, but consulted Charles by a ook.

"Do not forget that you are a daughter of the lood royal of Spain," said the old duke. "Do not orget what is due to the king your brother."

"I am not likely to forget what is due either to nyself or to the king," rejoined the Infanta, roudly.

And she gave her hand to the old duke, who ook it with the most profound respect, and delivered her to Doña Elvira, who by this time had ome up.

He then turned to Charles, and, making as deep reverence as that he had just addressed to the nfanta, said, in accents of grave respect,

"Your highness will be pleased to excuse me. n the discharge of my office as governor of the ady Infanta, I must entreat your highness to reire. I shall have the honour of attending you to he garden gate."

Charles did not return the old duke's salutation, but, regarding him with a lofty look, said,

"I shall use my own pleasure as to leaving the garden, my lord duke."

"Be not offended with me, noble prince," remonstrated the old duke. "Under any other circumstances, I would entreat your highness to remain here as long as might be agreeable to you—indeed, as his majesty's representative, I would place this garden and palace at your disposal—but I beseech you now to depart."

"No more, my lord duke," rejoined Charles, coldly. "I have said that I shall consult my own pleasure as to the time and mode of my departure."

"Prince," cried the duke, casting himself at Charles's feet, "I am an old man—old enough to be your grandsire—and my long life has been free from reproach. I am also head of the oldest and proudest family of Castile, whose scutcheon is without stain. Do not bring disgrace and dishonour upon me. Do not let it be said that I neglected my trust. The Infanta is confided to my care, and I am answerable for her with my head. I do not blame your highness for the rash step you have just taken, because you have been incited to it by overpowering passion, which has blinded you to the consequences."

"What are the consequences, my lord duke?" said Charles, still maintaining a haughty and inflexible deportment.

"Death and dishonour to me, prince," replied the duke—"punishment little less severe to Doña Elvira—immurement in a convent to the Lady Infanta—and a certain rupture between his majesty and your highness."

"Tut! tut! you magnify the matter, my lord," said Charles, incredulously.

"Highness," rejoined the old duke, in a sad and reproachful voice, "the word of Juan Hurtado de Mendoza has never yet been doubted. By my father's soul, I speak the truth! Were my own life merely in jeopardy, I would urge you no further. But wrong will be done to others far greater than myself. The Infanta will suffer—the king himself suffer—all the grandees of Spain will suffer by this violation of Spanish etiquette. Were he so minded, his majesty could not pass over the injury to his honour."

"No injury has been done to the king's honour, duke," said Charles. "I am the Infanta's suitor. Her hand has been promised me by his majesty. She herself has accepted me. I seek a momentary interview with her in private. I obtain it—that is all."

"Heaven keep all knowledge of the interview from my royal master!" cried the duke. "From me he shall never hear of it. As I have affirmed, he must resent it. Our nice sense of honour requires that no Castilian princess of the blood shall ex-

hange a word in private with the suitor for her
and until after their espousals. This rule your
ighness has infringed. But I beseech you to re-
ect—for your own sake—for the sake of the In-
nta—before you make the consequences of the
ep irretrievable."

"Rise, I pray you, my lord duke," said Charles,
using him. "You have convinced me. I see the
rror I have committed. I thank you for the de-
otion you have displayed to the Infanta—to my
ture consort. I will do as you desire."

"Nobly decided, prince," said the old duke.

While the Duke del Infantado had been thus
leading with the prince, the Infanta remained
anding at a little distance with Doña Elvira,
esisting all the attempts of the latter to induce
er to withdraw. She now stepped towards them,
nd with great dignity of manner said to the duke,

"My lord, after what has passed between you
nd the prince relative to my brief interview with

his highness, I think it right to tell you that we have plighted our faith, and that I regard him as my husband."

"You have not the power so to plight yourself, princess," rejoined the duke, "and therefore the promise is not binding."

"You are mistaken, my lord," said the Infanta, haughtily; "my promise is inviolable. I will wed no other than Charles Stuart, unless he himself shall discharge me from my pledge."

"Do not deceive yourself, princess," said the old duke, "and do not mislead the prince. Unless such promises are solemnly ratified, and by the consent of the king your brother, they are of no account."

"I hold *my* promise sacred, my lord duke," cried Charles, "and I call upon you to attest it."

"Mine is equally sacred. Bear witness to my words, my lord," added the Infanta.

"I hear—I hear," exclaimed the duke, with some impatience, "but I tell you the king would old such promises as nought, were they reported him, which they never will be by me, for my ps will remain always sealed in regard to this eeting. That you may be speedily united is my eartfelt wish, and that no impediment may arise that consummation of all our hopes, I would ge his highness's immediate departure.'

"Yes, you must go, prince—indeed you must," ied the Infanta. "So far the duke is right. If u are discovered, my brother will be so offended at I tremble for the consequences to us all. dios!"

She then tripped towards Doña Elvira, and, ving joined her, hurried along the path leading the casa. After proceeding to some distance, aria turned and perceived the prince still standg where she had left him, watching her. It ing evident that he would not stir as long as e continued in sight, she waved an adieu to n, and turned into a side-path.

"I am ready now, my lord," said Charles, as the Infanta disappeared.

Not a word passed between them as they pursued their way, following the course of the wall that bounded the garden, but when at last they reached the gate, the old duke said,

"I shall take no precautions, feeling assured your highness will not attempt to scale this garden wall again."

"Have no fear, my lord duke," replied Charles. "I shall not repeat the visit."

The gate was then unlocked, and Charles passed through it. Shortly afterwards he was joined by Buckingham and Gondomar, who were waiting for him.

END OF VOL. II.

LONDON:
PRINTED BY C. WHITING, BEAUFORT HOUSE, STRAND.

Milton Keynes UK
Ingram Content Group UK Ltd.
UKHW012215020224
437193UK00004B/143

9 781020 634093